BAD BLOOD

M. MALONE

BAD BLOOD © November 2018 M. Malone

Edited by Angie Ramey

CrushStar Romance

An Imprint of CrushStar Multimedia LLC

Print ISBN: 978-1-938789-67-0

Ebook ISBN: 978-1-938789-66-3

Contents

Chapter 1	1
Chapter 2	16
Chapter 3	28
Chapter 4	40
Chapter 5	54
Chapter 6	64
Chapter 7	78
Chapter 8	88
Chapter 9	99
Chapter 10	110
Chapter 11	122
Chapter 12	133
Chapter 13	146
Chapter 14	156
Chapter 15	168
Chapter 16	170
Chapter 17	173
Chapter 18	175
Epilogue	187
Epilogue	194
Also by M. Malone	215
About the Author	217

Bad Blood

Georgina Kingsley is off-limits. It's better this way, really. Her brother is my best friend and business partner, the closest thing I have to family. Plus, she's engaged to another man, one better for her than I could ever be.

But when Georgie is ditched on her wedding day, she needs someone to get her out of town. There's bad blood between us, but I'd do anything for her.

Except give her hot, rebound sex to get back at her cheating ex.

Tough choice. Loyalty to my best friend who has been more like a brother? Or to a woman with a history of driving me crazy and making me want things I have no right to ask for?

It's a hell of a time to realize I'm in love.

*Bad Blood is the fifth book in the LEFT AT THE ALTAR series, in a collaboration of six NYT Bestselling Authors: J. S. Scott, Ruth Cardello, Raine Miller, Sawyer Bennett, Minx Malone, and Melody Anne.

Chapter 1

*a*s Georgina Kingsley stared at her reflection, she thought it should be impossible to feel anything other than beautiful when wearing your wedding dress.

Her mother floated nervously around her, fussing with her veil and adjusting her train. Meanwhile she stared at the bride in the mirror, trying to find recognition there. But all she could see was a young woman who looked faintly like she was about to be sick.

"Stop making that face, Georgina. You'll get a crease in your forehead."

Acutely aware of the other women in the room watching them, Georgie held her tongue. Not for the first time she wished she'd fought harder to have who she really wanted in the wedding party.

She could blame that one on her older brother though. King hadn't been smart enough to meet his girlfriend Olivia until after the wedding preparations were almost complete and the wedding party already set.

It would have been so nice to have Olivia here to reassure her instead of feeling like she couldn't speak her mind. She had no idea if the women in the room were actually her real friends or not. The maid of honor was Alex's sister, Audrey, so she definitely couldn't confide her fears to her.

Ever since college, she'd grown apart from her old crowd. They were able to catch up now and then on social media, but Alex didn't like it when she traveled without him and always seemed jealous of the time she spent with anyone other than him.

He always said he loved her so much that he wanted her all to himself. In the beginning, his possessiveness had seemed kind of romantic.

Now, not so much.

Finally happy with the minute adjustments she'd made to the back of the dress, her mother put her arm around her and squeezed.

"Look at you. Our little girl is all grown up and an absolutely beautiful bride. I'm so proud of you." A chorus of voices chimed in, echoing her mother's words.

Part of her wanted to ask where was her mother's pride when Georgie got her degree? Or when she'd started her own business?

But after a lifetime as the daughter of Thane and Fiona Kingsley, she already knew where that conversation would lead.

"Is it almost time?"

Her mother glanced at the clock on the wall and nodded, suddenly frantic again. "Let me just go make sure that everything is on track."

After she was gone, Georgie was suddenly hit with another bout of nerves. But she was ready. She'd been with Alex since college. It wasn't an unusual story, she supposed. They'd dated for two years. He'd proposed at their graduation party. They'd had a tasteful yearlong engagement and were now getting married in a lavish ceremony on the grounds of her parents' ten-acre Northern Virginia estate.

According to her mother, the Summerlands were a bit too "new money" to be completely acceptable. However, after Georgie's rebellious phase in high school where she'd lived to torment her mother with dramatic hair dye, too much makeup and talk of being single, Fiona was probably just grateful Georgina was getting married at all.

She smoothed a stray curl behind her ear and listened to the faint sounds of the harpist whom Regina, the wedding planner, had insisted on. It was normal to be nervous before walking down an aisle in front of three hundred people. It didn't have anything to do with Alex. They had a great relationship and got along better than almost any other couple she knew.

Maybe it wasn't the wild, passionate affair she'd dreamed of as a teenager, but Alex was a good guy with a great career ahead of him working as a business management consultant for his father's company.

Everything about her wedding day had been planned and coordinated down to the tiniest detail. It was perfect.

So why was she fighting the urge to tear this stupid veil off her head and run away?

"Can I get you anything? Water? Do you need to use the bathroom? We can hold your dress up for you." Audrey tugged on the bodice of her dress.

The maid of honor wore a slightly different design than the other bridesmaids, but all of the dresses were a deep rose color. Or at least Regina said it was deep rose. To Georgie, it looked like eggplant.

She'd never liked eggplant.

"No, I think I'm fine for now. Thank you for everything you've done to help us get ready for the wedding. And for my bridal shower."

Audrey squeezed her arm. "Of course. We're family now. Summerlands stick together."

Her words echoed in Georgie's mind. She was going to be a Summerland.

Georgina Summerland.

Suddenly, she shivered.

"Are you cold?" Audrey asked. "I'll go see if I can find the thermostat. It is a little chilly in here."

A knock sounded at the door before it opened. Her mother came back in, with Regina following close behind. The wedding planner's mouth was twisted into her usual sour expression.

Georgie immediately felt guilty for the catty thought. Regina was a little... strong in her opinions, but she was one of Fiona's best friends and had done a phenomenal job planning the wedding. She just wished the other woman had been a bit more open to hearing her ideas. But what did she know? Apparently the wedding wasn't really for the bride. It was for her parents and all the people they wanted to impress.

"Audrey, what is that hideous thing?" Regina shouted, clutching her clipboard tighter.

Audrey froze and looked down uncertainly at the sweater in her hands. "Georgie was cold so–"

"It's black. It'll shed all over her dress." Regina snatched the offending sweater and handed it off to one of the bridesmaids. "Twenty minutes everyone!"

The announcement sent the previously calm room into a tailspin with women adjusting their stockings, hurrying to put on one more coat of mascara and fixing their hair. Since she couldn't risk messing up the train of her gown, Georgie couldn't do anything other than allow the chaos to swirl around her.

"Mom, can you make sure Dad isn't at the bar? You know how he gets when he's nervous."

Her mother stood immediately. "Yes, I'd better check. I'm sure he's a bit emotional about giving his baby girl away."

She turned to Audrey. "Can you check that all of the groomsmen are in place? They had their bachelor party last night so hopefully no one is missing or too hung over."

Audrey nodded, suddenly looking like a drill sergeant now that she had a mission.

One by one, Georgie asked each of the bridesmaids to check on something different just to buy herself some time alone. Even though they meant well, she couldn't think with all the other women chattering around her. And she needed to think.

Because she only had twenty minutes until her life changed forever.

———

*J*ames Hamilton, III stalked down the hallway following his best friend, King. It was a true testament to their friendship that he was present for the wedding of King's little sister.

He was the *last* person who should be there.

There was the obvious truth that he hated weddings. They were expensive, overblown affairs so that people could flaunt how much money they had in a socially acceptable way. He'd been married before and had known almost immediately that it was a mistake.

But more importantly, there was his complete and utter inability to be happy for the people getting married. Alex

Summerland was a dick, and he didn't deserve to marry anyone, let along Georgina Kingsley.

The only consolation in this fucked-up situation was that he knew he wasn't alone in his thoughts. King had been ranting ever since the prior night when they'd both endured the agony of attending Alex's bachelor party. It was apparently considered good etiquette to invite the male members of the bride's family, but Jamie had never been able to figure out who the hell thought that was a great idea.

Yes, invite your bride's family members to watch the groom get drunk and grind all over half-naked strippers. Sounds like a grand idea.

Just more evidence that the entire wedding industry was a farce.

His phone vibrated in his pocket. Annoyed, he pulled it out and made a face when he saw it was another voicemail.

"What's wrong?" King asked.

"It's just my parents again. Helen and Jim being Helen and Jim."

To anyone else that wouldn't make sense, but King understood. After spending so many holidays with the Kingsleys, his friend had wanted to know why they never visited Jamie's parents, so he finally invited King to the modest brick rancher in south New Jersey where he'd grown up.

His father had spent the entire visit trying to convince his son's *"rich friend"* to invest in his new business idea to sell inflatable beer cozies.

He had never taken King home again.

"How long has it been now?" King growled.

His grumpiness made Jamie smile, despite the circumstances. No matter how pissed off he was at the situation, he wasn't as mad as King.

"The ceremony should start in about ten minutes."

"If it starts on time," King muttered. "Maybe she'll change her mind."

"I doubt it won't start on time. There is a very scary woman with a clipboard walking around barking orders at people. I'm pretty sure if anyone is off schedule, she has a whip handy."

A man walked by wearing a tuxedo. Jamie figured he must be one of the groomsmen. It hit him then that another tradition was for the siblings of the bride and groom to both be in the wedding party.

"How did you get out of serving as a groomsman? Did Alex ask you?"

King shrugged. "He asked. I said no."

His tone of voice indicated that was all that was needed. If his face looked anything like it did now when Alex had asked, Jamie doubted anyone would be foolish enough to ask again.

King had always been very protective of his little sister and it didn't sit well with him at all that she was marrying so young and to someone that he didn't approve of.

Not that there was anything overtly wrong with Alex Summerland. And King didn't care about how new his family's money was the way his parents did. To King, money was money and all that mattered was whether you were smart enough to keep earning it.

A huge part of why they got along.

No, the reason King didn't like Alex was because the guy didn't seem all that into Georgie. When they were together, Alex was often talking to everyone else around her and didn't spare much attention for his bride-to-be at all. He didn't act like a man who was head-over-heels in love.

King saw it, and he wasn't the only one. Jamie shared his feelings about Alex, although not for the same reasons as his best friend. His reasons were much less altruistic.

He hated Alex Summerland because the man had the one thing Jamie wanted and could never have.

Georgie.

King was vaguely aware of his feelings, in the way that best friends often knew things about each other without discussing them outright. But there was also an unspoken understanding between them that certain things were off-limits. It was a known fact among men that you didn't mess with each other's mothers, sisters or close friends. As many women as there were in the world, no guy needed to fuck a woman related to a friend.

And they both knew that with Jamie, it would just be fucking. He didn't know how to do anything else, even if he'd wanted to. King knew his depraved taste better than almost anyone. Hell, he'd had a front row seat to most of it. They were very much alike. And the last thing King would ever want was for Georgie to end up with a guy like them.

"There you are, King." They both turned at the sound of Mrs. Kingsley's voice. "Darling, your father is having a bit of a moment. Can you go and talk to him? He's down at the bar. And don't let him have any more brandy."

Fiona Kingsley, although the mother to three children, never looked a day older than thirty-nine and kept her ice-blond hair in a sharp bob. She'd been like a second mother to him, which basically meant she felt free to nag Jamie the same way she did King.

"And Jamie, thank goodness you're here. I need someone to check in with the groom and make sure he has everything he needs. They're in the study."

"I'm not really sure–"

She patted his cheek. "Thank you, darling."

His jaw ached as he clamped his teeth together. He knew coming to the wedding had been a mistake and now he was being sent right into the heart of the fire. Jamie walked in the direction Fiona pointed, resolved to his fate. King had already walked off, and he definitely wasn't going to go sit outside with the other guests.

It was one of those errands that women sent men on because it made them feel better. It was doubtful anyone in the groom's party actually needed anything. What could a guy need before getting married? All they had to do was show up, wear their tux, and make sure they had the ring.

As a matter of fact, maybe he would take this opportunity to slip out. Jamie had already been seen by everyone he cared about, so he could easily leave and no one would ever be the wiser. In fact, King's father had the right idea. As soon as he turned the corner, he changed course.

Hitting the bar before he left sounded like as good an idea as any.

As he walked back down the hall, one of the doors opened and Georgie's face appeared.

"Psst. Hey, Jamie!"

Despite everything he couldn't resist a chuckle. Georgie was so animated that King used to tell everyone she was his pet terrier and not to feed her treats because it made her hyper. Jamie had always enjoyed her antics, even though he knew her mother in particular was always trying to get her to be more demure, more ladylike.

Or something like that.

"You rang?"

"What are you doing here?" She glared at him suspiciously.

"It's in the guy code handbook that you must attend family weddings. Even if it's for your best friend's bratty little sister."

"Oh, har-har-har. You're such a comedian. Really you're just here to pick up bridesmaids."

Jamie chuckled evilly. "That's not the reason. But it's definitely a reward."

If it were possible for steam to come out of someone's ears in anything other than a cartoon, he would have expected to see smoke streaming from her ears. Georgie poked him in the stomach right beneath the ribs.

"Ow! What the hell? That hurt."

"Good. Maybe it'll remind you to stay away from my bridesmaids! One of them is my future sister-in-law."

"Is she hot?"

"Jamie!"

"I'm joking. No boinking bridesmaids. No sexing up the sister-in-law. This wedding is boring already."

"You'd better behave."

"Or what? What are you going to do? Tell the scary clipboard lady on me? Although I admit she is kind of terrifying."

Georgie grinned. "I might have to accidentally sign you up for Furniture Barn emails again. Enjoy your spam."

He stopped laughing. "Brat. The tech department had to give me a new laptop last time you did that."

"Just leave Audrey alone."

He held up his hands. "She's not my type anyway."

"I thought your type was female. Breathing. Preferably blond."

"Surprisingly, I have a thing for mouthy brunettes. Ones that look like heaven and probably taste like sin."

Jamie wasn't sure what made him say it. It was completely inappropriate considering it was her wedding day and all. But there was something about that smart mouth that made him forget all the rules.

He leaned closer until he could hear the little gasp she made. "You look beautiful, Georgie. Alex is a lucky bastard."

Then he walked away before he did something truly crazy. Like tell her not to get married. To give him a chance instead.

Chapter 2

*A*lone again, Georgie took several deep breaths and did the visualization exercises she'd read about in a self-help book the prior week. With her eyes closed, she imagined a beautiful white sand beach and colorful drinks with little umbrellas in them. Her heart rate slowed finally as she thought of the gorgeous resort they would be flying to the next day.

All she had to do was get through the ceremony and the reception.

And somehow manage to forget about Jamie's parting words. He'd never said anything like that to her before. Jamie either treated her like an annoying little sister the same way King did or ignored her completely.

He'd certainly never looked at her like *that*.

James Hamilton III, also known as Jamie to everyone other than her uptight brother, was usually just a royal pain in her ass.

Her face heated as she remembered the last time she'd seen him. A few months ago, Georgie had done something a little crazy. She'd discovered her brother's girlfriend owned an exclusive sex club and she'd asked Olivia to get her in. Not because she wanted to actually do anything there but just out of curiosity.

Georgie sniffed. People acted like it was such a big deal if a woman wanted to explore her options a bit. Was it really so wrong to wonder if sex was supposed to be so... boring?

She winced. It felt disloyal to even think it, but the truth was that sex wasn't something she looked forward to about married life. Alex was very traditional, which translated to polite missionary sex every Saturday night. Georgie had just wanted to see what it was like for people who weren't afraid to branch out a little. No big deal. She'd been perfectly safe until Jamie barged in and dragged her out in front of everyone.

She'd never been so humiliated.

For months, she hadn't been able to look him in the eye. Although she shouldn't have been the one embarrassed. He should have been embarrassed about sticking his way too good-looking nose where it didn't belong.

Determined to forget about it, she carefully unfolded the note she'd written for Alex on her signature pink stationery. Her business, *Sweet Nothings*, was a unique greeting card service that delivered handwritten notes and cards for special occasions. She had agonized over what to write for Alex on their wedding day. Finally, she'd decided to keep it simple.

Forever starts today.

I love you.

Georgie

Her hands shook slightly as she refolded the note and tucked it into the matching envelope. It was an old tradition for wives and husbands to exchange gifts on their wedding day, one that most people didn't bother with anymore. But Georgie had always thought it was sweet and wanted Alex to have something unique and personal from her rather than a store-bought gift. She'd decorated the envelope with little hand-drawn wedding images like a wedding dress, a tuxedo and a bouquet of flowers. She thought it was a nice touch, although Alex probably wouldn't notice.

Alex didn't notice a lot of things.

Georgie placed a hand over her suddenly churning stomach. Nerves were normal, but she was starting to panic. Maybe if she could see Alex and talk to him, this horrible feeling that she was making a mistake would go away.

Regina would have a fit if she asked to be taken to where the men were getting ready. That wasn't in the plan, and God forbid they do anything that wasn't on Regina's to-do list.

Screw this, she thought and walked over to the door. Pulling it open, she peered into the hallway.

No one would know if she snuck away to see Alex for a bit before the ceremony. Sure, there was that old tradition about it being bad luck for the bride and groom to see each other before the wedding, but they weren't superstitious people. She'd been raised by a businessman, and her debutante mother was just as cunning as her father.

Their home had several wings, and she knew exactly where her mother had put Alex. He was in her father's office. Several of the cleaning staff bustled by before she reached the door to her father's domain.

This room had always held special memories for her. No matter how busy her father might have been, he'd always had time for a hug, and he used to let her play on the floor while he was on the phone or working at his desk.

Laughter and voices greeted her as she pulled the door open slightly. She was hardly a wedding expert, hers had been planned by her mother and Regina, but she assumed the groom's party was all in there with him getting dressed. The last thing she wanted was to surprise anyone and then have to get through the entire ceremony with naked groomsmen on the brain.

But when she peeked in, she didn't see anyone. Then she heard voices again. Alex and his father were over by the window talking. They hadn't seen her yet.

"Now that you've gotten in with the Kingsleys, we're going to be in a very good position going forward. Their contacts alone are worth millions."

Georgie paused in shock when she heard what Mr. Summerland was saying. Her hand curled around the doorknob. He'd always been very nice to her, inviting her over for dinner and telling her to say hi to her parents.

"We all have to make sacrifices," Alex replied. "Georgie will make a good wife. I would have had to settle down at some point anyway."

"Good way of thinking about it, son. Now if only I could get your brother on the same page." Mr. Summerland seemed annoyed that one of his offspring had his own ideas about life.

"Make him the right offer and he will be. You think I'd be getting married if you hadn't dangled the partnership carrot in front of me?"

Georgie's hand flexed on the doorknob, moving it slightly. Alex's laughter cut off when their gazes met. His eyes narrowed. "Georgie?"

She turned and fled. Her mind was racing with everything she'd just learned, but there was only one thing that stuck out in her mind.

She had to get out of there.

———

A half an hour later, the wedding still hadn't started, and Jamie was getting restless.

Yeah, yeah, he was supposed to be gone by now. But who could look away if they knew a train wreck was about to happen? It wasn't so easy to nonchalantly stroll in the other direction when someone he cared about was standing on the edge of a cliff and about to jump off.

He took another bracing sip of Macallan, enjoying the smooth texture and then the crisp bite at the end. Mr. Kingsley had always maintained a well-stocked bar. Something that he was grateful for now that they were stuck in this hell of waiting to find out what was going on.

"My baby girl can't get married. She used to sit in my office while I worked and play with her dolls. Now she's supposed to be someone's wife?"

Colin, the second oldest of the Kingsley siblings, kept his eyes on his phone. He was the only one with light brown hair, unlike Georgie and King who had their father's dark hair and blue eyes. He'd never gotten along with King, so he'd moved out as soon as he could and didn't spend much time with the rest of the family.

King glanced at his father's now empty glass and raised his eyebrows. Mrs. Kingsley had asked him to make sure his father didn't drink too much, but Mr. Kingsley was already three sheets to the wind by the time they found him. So technically it wasn't their fault. It was more like damage control at that point.

"I'm not sure what's holding things up. Mom is checking. Alex probably did something," King growled. "I swear if Georgie caught him fucking a bridesmaid or some other cliché shit, I will kill him."

"Me too!" Mr. Kingsley raised his glass in agreement, but his coordination was so off that he almost fell.

King caught his father and got him settled back on the stool before glancing over at Jamie. "You don't have to stick around, man. I know weddings aren't your thing. Didn't you have somewhere to be tonight?"

That was his perfect out. He was being handed an excuse to walk away from the train wreck, but he couldn't do it.

As perverse as it was, he needed to witness Georgina Kingsley walk down the aisle to a man who didn't deserve her. He needed to hear her perfect, pillowy lips utter the vows that would place her permanently out of reach. Maybe then his brain would stop entertaining impossible fantasies and he could finally get over it.

Although the fact that he'd seen her half-naked certainly didn't help with the fantasizing situation.

His brain immediately shut down that line of thought. Jamie couldn't think about Georgie naked while sitting next to her distraught father. That was just weird. And wrong.

And weird.

Besides, there hadn't been anything sexy about accidentally encountering Georgie at a sex club. King had gotten a membership to the exclusive Club VIP last year and ended up dating one of the owners. After realizing that his usual wingman was going out of commission, possibly forever, Jamie could freely admit that he was a little thrown. He'd gone back to the club to let off a little steam and relax.

Only he'd gotten way more than he bargained for when he ran into a scantily clad Georgie looking like a virgin sacrifice in a den of sinners.

"I'm going out of town tonight. Meeting up with an old friend."

King chuckled. "Yeah, I figured. You have more old friends than any man I know."

Normally Jamie would have laughed but somehow the joke made him feel worse. Just another reminder that King knew more about him than anyone else. The good, the bad, and the really fucking ugly.

"I'll stay a little longer. Just in case you need my help rearranging Alex's face or anything."

King grunted in approval at that. But before he could respond, Mrs. Kingsley ran up looking harried.

"Georgie is missing! We've looked everywhere. No one knows where she is."

King stood immediately. "I'll check the attic. Maybe she got cold feet and decided to hide out up there."

Mr. Kingsley staggered to his feet unsteadily. "Maybe she's in the pool house." Colin followed his father.

Unsure how to help, Jamie volunteered to check all the guest rooms upstairs. As he walked through the expansive family room, he could see outside to the back lawn where the guests were waiting. Seeing that long white runner going up the aisle to the altar really brought it home.

Georgie was missing from her own wedding and there weren't too many ways this could end well.

The guest rooms upstairs all proved to be empty, as he'd figured they would. His fascination with Georgina meant that over the years he'd spent a lot of time watching her at social events. Unlike the others, he knew Georgie had a long history of hiding out when she was nervous or scared.

King and the rest of his family were outgoing extroverts that loved parties and socializing. Georgie played the role well, the result of a lifetime of practice. But he could tell when she was faking it, and when she got uncomfortable, she would usually disappear from the event only to reappear much later.

It had become like a game for him, to predict when she would sneak out and see if he could catch her. He'd followed her a couple of times to find her raiding the pantry, an area that the rest of the family rarely used.

The Kingsleys were *stupid* rich, the kind that most people only saw on television or in movies. They had year-round, live-in staff so they never went in their pantry. If they got hungry, they called for someone to bring them food.

Making the pantry the perfect hiding spot.

Of course.

Jamie turned abruptly and retraced his steps. He skipped down the stairs and walked back across the family room. The entrance to the servant's wing was through a set of double doors and down a hallway. As he walked, the sounds behind him became more muted. Most everyone was outside, roaming the house carrying out tasks for Fiona or on the other side of the lawn making preparations for the reception.

He looked around the corner and then waited until one of the waiters left the kitchen. Then he crossed to the pantry door and pulled it open.

Empty.

His heart sank until he noticed a rice bag moved awkwardly in the middle of the floor. Jamie walked forward and then looked behind it and into the far-right corner. Georgie was sitting directly on the floor, her arms curled around her knees.

The long train of her gown was hitched up behind her, making it look like she was sitting in the middle of a huge scoop of whipped cream.

He wasn't going to be the guy who started with the obvious questions. Something was wrong, and she didn't want to be found. So he got right to the point.

"Do you want to get out of here?"

Chapter 3

eorgie looked up warily when she heard footsteps. Was Jamie coming back or had someone else found her?

She'd come down here to hide because no one would ever look for her in the pantry. After what she'd overheard, she hadn't wanted to go back to her room and smile and pretend everything was perfect.

But everywhere she turned, she saw something that reminded her of the wedding. Decorations, flowers, people.

So many people.

It had driven home what was at stake. This was no small thing. There were three hundred people outside waiting for her to marry Alex, and she wasn't sure she could do it.

The pantry door opened, and she tensed until she recognized the distinct scent of Jamie. The man always smelled amazing. Not that she followed him around sniffing like a weirdo, but considering how often he was at the house to visit King, it was almost impossible to avoid being in close contact with him.

"I wasn't able to get into your room since everyone is there, so I got my gym bag from my car. The T-shirt will be huge on you, but it'll do for now."

She stood, placing one hand on the wall and the other on his shoulder so she didn't fall as she maneuvered around her huge train. As she looked at the clothes in his hand, heat started climbing her neck. How could she have forgotten the dress?

"I'm going to need your help to get out of this thing."

As his face paled, her humiliation doubled. "Never mind. I'll just go back upstairs. I'm probably overreacting anyway."

His head snapped up. "You're not overreacting. You're the sweetest person I know. If you're upset, then you have reason to be."

His praise pleased her way more than it should have. Jamie was known for being direct and exacting. Not the type of man to give out praise easily so if he said something, he meant it. And he wasn't easy to impress. Something about the way he said it made it seem like he not only approved of her but also maybe... liked her, too. A surprise, since he usually seemed annoyed by her. Something that hurt her feelings although she'd never admit it.

She straightened. *You don't need anyone's approval. That's what got you into this mess.*

"Thank you. I just want to get out of this thing and then I guess I have to go talk to Alex." She turned so he could start on the row of buttons on the back of her dress.

"You don't have to do a damn thing you don't want to do."

She couldn't see his face but felt the first tug as he started pushing the buttons through the holes.

"If only that were true," she whispered. But this whole incident had forced her to take a good, hard look at her life.

Now that her anger had cooled a bit, she saw the situation clearly. Her relationship with Alex wasn't a love match, and all the things she'd thought were wrong were warnings from her subconscious trying to tell her to wake up.

Well, she hadn't gotten the message until she'd actually heard it from the source, and where did that leave her?

All of her friends were also friends with Alex. Her entire life revolved around being the perfect future wife for him, and now she saw how much she'd truly lost. The only person who would take her in without a lot of questions was Olivia, King's girlfriend, but she was currently at the wedding along with the rest of her family.

She had nowhere to go.

"Tell me he didn't hurt you, Georgie."

Jamie's quiet, intense voice touched something deep inside. Something she wasn't ready to examine just yet.

"He didn't do any of the things you're imagining." She sighed. "He just doesn't love me."

Cool air bathed her back as the last button popped free and it was like breathing for the first time. She sucked in breath after breath until the room spun and she saw stars.

"Whoa. Take it easy." Jamie held her up when she slumped slightly.

"Sorry." Georgie couldn't look at him as she pulled down the sleeves of her dress.

"Shit. I'll... uh, I'm not looking."

The discomfort in his voice amused her, but there was no time to dwell on it. If Jamie had been sent to look for her, it meant she'd been down here feeling sorry for herself longer than she'd thought. It wouldn't be long before her mother finally asked one of the staff if they'd seen her, and then she'd be out of time.

"Okay, I'm ready."

The shirt fell to her knees, and the drawstring shorts hung dangerously loose on her hips even after she'd yanked and tied the string. But it wasn't the torture device she'd just been wearing so it would do.

Jamie put her dress in the corner behind the rice bag. "Let's put this out of the way just so no one steps on it when they come in here. I'm sure it's outrageously expensive."

"Yeah. Everything about this wedding was outrageously expensive. It was supposed to be a fairytale. I guess I wasn't supposed to overhear Alex's father congratulating him on locking down a successful business merger with the Kingsleys."

When Jamie glanced at her over his shoulder, she braced herself to see all the emotions she was expecting once everyone found out the wedding was off. Sympathy. Pity.

Poor Georgie, saved herself for the perfect man only to find out that perfect doesn't exist.

But there were none of those things reflected in Jamie's eyes. Only a shared outrage that made her lift her chin a little higher.

"Well, let's get the hell out of here and leave them all to wonder what happened to their business deal."

———

*J*amie opened the door to his Range Rover and waited while Georgie climbed in. He'd expected it to be harder to sneak her out of the house, but everyone had been upstairs or outside with the wedding guests.

No one had been interested in what was going on in the servant's wing. They'd just walked straight to the front door and out to his car.

He sent up a silent prayer of thanks that he had been late to arrive and didn't allow the valets to park his car. He was at the end of the Kingsley's long drive, along with other family members who'd taken the initiative to park themselves.

"Where to, princess?" The endearment slipped out before he could catch it. It was how he'd often thought of her, the perfect girl who was too good for the commoners around her.

Georgie's eyes betrayed her surprise, looking even more blue today due to whatever girl magic she'd done to her face. It was quite a sight to see her wearing a full face of makeup and his old gym clothes, but in typical Georgie fashion, she made it look good.

"I'm not sure. Where do you go when home isn't where you want to be? A hotel maybe?"

The way she asked the question made him sad for her. And angry. Nothing about this situation made any sense. Georgie shouldn't be running away in shame when she had done nothing wrong. Alex Summerland had been a lucky bastard and clearly batting out of his league. He should be the one slinking off into the shadows looking for somewhere to hide.

"I can take you to a friend's house. Although I guess most of your friends are probably here, huh?" He was beginning to see her dilemma.

Being a runaway bride was a lot easier in the movies. You just put your sneakers on and took off with your thumb stuck out. But here in the real world, someone like Georgie wouldn't get far without her wallet, phone, or car. Jamie was suddenly really glad he hadn't left. The thought of her hitchhiking scared the hell out of him, and even if she'd been able to get into the city, she didn't have any money for a hotel.

He didn't want to think about the kind of trouble a beautiful woman like Georgie could attract on her own.

"I'm not taking you to a hotel. There has to be somewhere we can go. What about King's place? You're on the approved guest list, so the concierge would let you up."

She shook her head. "No way. As soon as everyone realizes I'm gone, that's the first place they'll look. I'm just not ready to talk to anyone yet. I don't want to see the disappointment in their faces."

"Georgie..." His hands curled around the steering wheel as he drove, wishing there was something he could say to make it better.

But coming from a poor background, Jamie saw the truth of her life probably more clearly than she did. He'd had to learn to navigate a social class different from the one he was born into, which meant studying the super-rich like they were a new species he'd just discovered. The women in Georgie's world were expected, above all else, to marry well. It was utter bullshit, but it was also utterly true.

He wasn't going to lie to her and pretend her parents wouldn't be disappointed at this turn of events because they would be.

"Okay, not King's place then. Maybe we can just grab something to eat until you feel better. Then you can make a decision."

Georgie looked down at her clothes in horror. "Go out to eat. Like this?"

He chuckled. "You always look beautiful."

She gave him a *yeah right* look. "You're very sweet to lie to me like that. I'm more concerned that these shorts will fall down at any minute and I'll be mooning everyone. The last thing I need is more humiliation today."

She fell quiet, and Jamie didn't press her for a destination; he just drove. When he'd first started working with King, there had been days when everything around him seemed like it was going to shit, and he used to jump in his car and drive. He never had any particular destination. Sometimes it was enough to just be on the way somewhere. Somewhere other than where you didn't want to be.

"He doesn't love me, Jamie."

Georgie's voice was soft, but the hurt was so palpable that even Jamie felt it.

"He never loved me. And I think a part of me knew all along." She sniffed, and one hand came up to swipe at her cheek.

Jamie wished he hadn't spirited her away so quickly but instead taken the opportunity to punch Alex in the face before they'd left.

"He's an idiot. And I no longer have to feel guilty about all the shit King and I have talked about him behind his back."

She didn't say anything, just kept staring out the window and swiping at her cheeks every few minutes or so. He'd never felt so helpless or so useless than watching Georgie's heart break over someone who wasn't even worthy of her.

"The worst part is how I let him change me. How could I not see what he was doing? He was obviously trying to create the perfect robot wife to help him get his father's approval. This is the same man who at his last company holiday party told me I needed to behave with more *decorum*. That I was representing the Kingsleys, after all."

Jamie shook his head. "What a douchebag."

But Georgie wasn't done. She twisted in her seat and pointed one finger in the air as she continued her angry rant. "The man who made me feel like a whore for wanting to try a sexual position other than boring, basic missionary!"

He almost ran off the road at her pronouncement and had to yank the wheel to right their course.

"Um, okay. I think we've established that Alex sucked."

"Or didn't suck, as it turned out," Georgie grumbled.

Jamie snickered at that. "So many things I could say to that.

But I won't." Although he was inappropriately happy to find out her former fiancé hadn't ever satisfied her in bed.

So many things were starting to make sense. Finding Georgie wandering around a sex club had seemed so strange and out of character at the time. Like finding a clown in a funeral home. But now he could see why she'd gone there. Georgie was the curious type, always had been, and she'd probably thought going to the club was the easiest way to find out whether the problems in her sex life were universal or particular to Alex.

"Whatever, my point is that I came close to never finding out what it's like to really be happy in a relationship. That's what my life would have been if I'd married Alex."

His phone rang, and without looking at it, he silenced it.

"Shouldn't you get that?" she asked sadly. "It's probably my mother."

"Anyone who really cares about you already knows that you're safe."

"How?"

"I texted King right before we left. He can handle telling everyone else. Meanwhile you can hide out at my place."

"Your place? You don't have to babysit me, Jamie. I appreciate the ride, but this isn't your problem."

"It's the only place you can hide out where no one will come looking for you. And we can get something to eat without fear of you mooning anyone."

She snorted at his lame attempt at humor, but he could feel her questioning gaze long afterward.

He kept his eyes on the road. The last thing he needed was to deal with those baby blues staring straight through to his soul while he invented a reason he wanted to keep her close.

Because he wasn't sure why the hell he wanted her at his place either.

*a*n hour later, they were eating pizza sitting cross-legged on the floor in front of his TV. Pizza and a cheesy Lifetime movie were a poor substitute for what should have been the happiest day of her life, but Georgie hadn't complained once.

Although she had made herself at home by pouring several tequila shots at his wet bar. Not that he was judging.

Other than the tequila and the faint red in her eyes, Jamie would have never guessed she'd just gone through something traumatic. She wasn't behaving like a woman who'd just discovered her fiancé had only been marrying her for financial reasons.

Actually, she was handling it all a little *too* well. It was freaking him out.

"What's that?" he asked, noticing her attention had been captured by a small, pink envelope. There were little cartoon drawings on the outside, but he wasn't close enough to see what they were.

Georgie shrugged. "You remember my business?"

"Yeah. *Sweet Nothings*. How are things going with that?"

She stared at him. "You remember the name of my company?"

"Of course. You hounded me for weeks with all those questions about starting a company."

Her smile lit up the room. "You finally gave in just so I'd go away."

Jamie grunted, heat blooming in his cheeks. He turned away so she wouldn't see the truth in his eyes. He hadn't helped her so she'd go away. Quite the opposite. If anything, he'd taken shameless advantage of a legitimate reason to spend time with her.

Most of her questions about opening a business could have been answered in less than an hour but he'd dragged it out, milking his only chance to spend time alone with her without King or her parents as a buffer. And he'd been happy to do it. When Georgie was excited about something, it spilled out of her and blanketed everyone around her in joy. Jamie had loved every minute of basking in her radiance.

And when she was sad, it was as if a rain cloud was covering everything. Seeing her without a huge smile on her face was so foreign to him.

"You're sure you're okay? I can get King over here if you want. Or Olivia. Maybe she can keep you company while your brother and I go look for Alex."

She shook her head. "I'm sure King already had a talk with Alex. One that began and ended with a fist to the face."

"No, actually Alex disappeared shortly after you did. King said when he went looking for him no one could find him."

Which was weird. He wondered what exactly had happened before he'd found Georgie curled up on the floor in that pantry. Had she had a fight with Alex? That would explain why he'd been nowhere to be found. Jamie glanced over at Georgie. *Shit.* He wasn't going to be the one to ask her.

"So, the pink envelope is a business thing?" he finally said.

"It's our signature. We use pink envelopes for all our custom greetings and notes. Anyway, I wrote a special note for Alex. I was supposed to give it to him after the ceremony, but I went to see him beforehand. That's when I overheard him talking to his father about the partnership he was promised in exchange for marrying a Kingsley."

Jamie sighed. She'd gone to see her fiancé to give him something she'd written just for him only to have it all blow up in her face. Life really wasn't fair sometimes.

"I'm sorry, Georgie."

Her eyes were bright when they next met his. "Don't be. At least I found out before the wedding. Otherwise I would have been just one more person divorced within a year of getting married. It's funny that the owner of a love letter business can't even find a happily ever after. I spent so long waiting for the perfect guy only to find out perfect doesn't exist."

"No, it doesn't."

"He was my first," Georgie whispered before resting her head on her arm.

Unsure of how to respond, Jamie stood and walked over to the wet bar. Clearly, she'd had the right idea from the start. There was no way in hell he was getting through this conversation without scotch. The thought of her being with Alex made him want to throw something.

An image of a teenage Georgie looking up at him with adoration and desire pushed itself into his mind.

Thanks a lot brain, he thought. *Keep reminding me of every mistake I've ever made.*

If he hadn't pushed her away years ago, he would have been her first. He would have been the one to touch that soft skin and kiss those pouty lips. But then that would make him the asshole instead of Alex because he wasn't any better for her.

"At least now I know why our sex life was so lackluster," Georgie moaned.

He took a bracing sip of the scotch he'd just poured, not bothering to look at the label. It didn't really matter other than as a way to get through this.

"You know what really kills me?" Georgie waved her shot glass in the air as she made her point. "That he always made me feel bad for wanting to try things. Some of us don't want to have boring missionary sex every Saturday. Maybe it'd be nice to get fucked on a Wednesday. Imagine that!"

The second sip of scotch slid down the wrong pipe and Jamie dissolved into a coughing fit. He pounded his chest trying to clear the burn from his windpipe.

"*Jesus,* Georgie."

"What? I'm just saying. Would you want to be stuck having sex once a week in the same position? With the lights off," she added before rolling her eyes.

Damn, that really did sound boring as hell.

Jamie shook his head hard, trying to clear the weirdness of having this conversation in the first place and also to stop himself from noticing how adorable she was while tipsy and ranting.

"You deserve a man who cherishes you. Who will put you first and not push you to do things that are out of your comfort zone like going to sex clubs. That isn't you."

Georgie cracked up. "God, you're such a guy. You've convinced yourself the big bad wolf corrupted me somehow. But it was *my* idea to go to the sex club, Jamie. I'm the one who wanted to try something new. No one influenced me to take a walk on the wild side."

Jamie had no idea what to say to that. He could freely admit that he'd assumed she'd only gone to the club because Alex was pressuring her into trying new things. It had never occurred to him that she'd really been there of her own volition. And yes, he realized that made him a total hypocrite. But this was Georgie.

"Speaking of that night–" she began.

"Let's not actually," Jamie interrupted.

He spun around to face the other direction before she could see the monster erection pressing against his slacks.

"Um, all I was going to say was that I understand what you were trying to do that night. But I don't need a keeper. I'm a grown woman and if I want to go to a sex club, I can. As a matter of fact, maybe I'll go back now that I've found out the truth about Alex."

"The hell you will," Jamie growled, finally turning to face her again. "That's not the kind of place for idle curiosity, Georgie. I'm not saying that to be a dick or spoil your fun or whatever. Some of the stuff going on there is pretty hardcore."

Her face was mutinous and set in the expression he'd come to recognize over the years as her *I'll do what I want* face. Even though it was inconvenient, he was glad to see that Alex hadn't squished all the spunk and defiance out of her.

"I shouldn't have brought it up. I'm sure you don't want to talk about my stupid problems."

He really didn't. But he *did* want her to have someone to talk to if she needed it. "It's okay. You have the right to vent."

Georgie shook her head. "I know you're doing this as a favor to King. You've always been such a good friend to him. But no guy wants to hear about sex from a girl who is like a little sister to him."

Just like that all the latent sexual tension he'd been holding back boiled over. Between the crowbar in his pants and the mental images of her in that damn sex club, it all proved to be more than Jamie could take.

He abandoned his glass on the bar and stalked back over to where Georgie was sprawled on the floor. Her eyes followed his movements warily. He kneeled next to her and put one finger gently under her chin. "Let's get one thing straight, princess."

"What's that?" she whispered.

"You are not my fucking sister." Then his mouth covered hers.

———

*G*eorgie was in shock. Either that or she'd already passed out and was now hallucinating this whole thing. But even if it was an alcohol-induced dream, she planned to enjoy it. Because Jamie was kissing her, and she'd been dreaming about this for years.

Her initial shock gave way and she wrapped a hand around his neck to pull him down. She moaned as she got lost in the taste and smell of him, wanting nothing more than to crawl into his lap and stay all night.

But before she could make good on the wish, Jamie was pulling away. "*Shit*. That shouldn't have happened."

Stunned, Georgie just stared at him. "But... you don't even like me."

The look Jamie gave her could have melted steel. "I have always liked you, Georgie. It's pretty damn hard not to."

She snorted. "You didn't like me too much when you dragged me out of that club."

His eyes narrowed. "I wanted to spank your sexy little ass for that stunt. For months, I couldn't get the image of you in that corset out of my head. The sight of your perky little breasts pushed up and pointing right at me is one of my favorite personal fantasies."

Georgie knew her mouth was hanging open but couldn't help it. Clearly she wasn't the only one who'd lost the filter tonight because she would have never guessed that Jamie had those kinds of thoughts about her.

"Personal fantasies?" she whispered. Was he talking about...

"Yeah, princess. I gave my right hand quite a workout after you pulled that little stunt. God, you were so fucking wasted on Alex."

For some reason, his anger at her being with Alex only made

the ache between her legs grow. Georgie squirmed at the idea of him stroking one out to the memory of her in lingerie. Her mouth was suddenly dry as her imagination raced with images of Jamie holding his cock in his hand, tugging on it while he thought about her.

"That's why I went to the club. I just wanted to see if I could feel–"

Suddenly she glanced up at him and the air around them became charged. Her entire existence narrowed to the way Jamie was looking at her right then.

"Feel like what?" he prompted, his eyes intense.

"The way I do when you look at me." Her lip trembled as the words finally tumbled out. Then she leaned up and pressed her lips against his.

Instinct took over and suddenly who they were didn't matter. He wasn't a guy comforting his best friend's little sister, and she wasn't the heartbroken bride. Right then, their entire world was her lips against his and how astonishingly perfect it was.

Georgie moaned when his hand speared through her hair to cradle her head and pull her closer. Lights sparked behind her eyelids when his tongue snaked out to tentatively touch hers. Everything about him aroused her from his strength to the clean rugged scent of his skin.

Sex with him wouldn't be a weekly chore.

It would be an experience.

As soon as the idea bloomed, she started tugging at his dress shirt. Buttons popped off and scattered across the floor as her hands pushed beneath the fabric searching for his skin.

"Whoa, Georgie. Slow down."

"Don't want to slow down. I want you, Jamie."

His tortured groan only increased her urgency.

"Georgie," he whispered, turning his head slightly to keep his lips away from temptation. "We shouldn't be doing this."

"Why? Because I'm goody-two-shoes Georgie? The girl who never has any fun?"

He tapped her nose. "No. Because I care about you too much to take you to bed for a night. You deserve more than that."

"Maybe I don't want more than that. For once, I want to do the irresponsible, impulsive fun thing. Life is short, and I want to have wild, crazy sex that makes me forget about the years I wasted on Alex."

"Revenge sex?"

Georgie huffed out a frustrated breath. "What's wrong with that? If I'd made a few mistakes before getting engaged, then I would have known something was off about my relationship."

Jamie hung his head. "I must have done something really bad in a past life."

"What?" Confused, Georgie could only stare as he set her aside carefully and stood.

"Nothing. Just that this is cruel and unusual punishment." He walked into the kitchen and then came back with a glass of ice water. "Drink this. Then text your brother. Otherwise he'll end up coming here to check on you."

Then he walked down the hallway leading to the bedrooms.

While he was gone, Georgie reluctantly drank the water and thought about what had just happened. She'd never seen him like that. Out of control and uninhibited. He was always so polite and distant that it drove her crazy.

But now it was like the outer layer of perfection he always wore like a mantle had been stripped away and his vulnerable underbelly was exposed.

She liked it.

But if his reaction afterward was any indication, she wouldn't be seeing it again. Despite his obvious physical reaction to her, he didn't seem nearly as interested in getting naked as she was.

When he finally returned, he was wearing a new shirt and looked perfectly composed.

She sighed. "So, I guess revenge sex is off the table then?"

He wouldn't meet her eyes. "That's correct."

Not that it should be a complete surprise. After all, she had a really embarrassing memory that proved she wasn't his type.

She'd always figured he tolerated her because of his close friendship with King not because of any real affection for her. He'd always seemed annoyed by her constant rambling.

The kiss was more than likely a result of timing and alcohol.

"I know, I know. Because I'm King's sister."

"No... okay, that's partially why but also because I'm here to make sure you're okay. Not... whatever that was."

She sighed. She really should be used to disappointment by now. Of course, Jamie hadn't kissed her because he'd secretly been pining for her. She knew his reputation with women. Kissing her had probably just been a reflex when seeing a girl crying and pitiful in his apartment. *She* was the one who'd dragged him closer. Now he was trying to let her down easy.

"You know what, let's just skip the whole *it's not you it's me* thing, okay?"

Funny, she wouldn't have thought her day could get any more embarrassing. But then she'd always been an overachiever.

Maximum mortification: Achieved

Chapter 5

*W*hen he got back home, it was quiet.

Too quiet.

Jamie turned on several lights and then some music for good measure. He was alone, but that was no different from any other night. There was no logical reason that his apartment should suddenly feel cold and empty.

He opened the refrigerator and the first thing he saw was the pizza he'd shared with Georgie. The one covered in pineapple that he thought was disgusting but he'd ordered because it made her happy.

He closed the refrigerator.

It was a Saturday night. Usually he'd be out on a date or catching up on some work. Jamie didn't believe in boredom.

Bored people were ones who either didn't have enough to do or any creativity to think of something to amuse themselves.

But he'd canceled his date as soon as things started going downhill at the wedding. And there was no way he could concentrate on work. His eyes would cross if he tried to read a profit and loss statement right then.

For the first time in ages, he was bored.

No, that was a lie. He wasn't bored. He was frustrated. Because he had free time, but he couldn't spend it doing what he wanted to do. Namely going back to that hotel and climbing into that huge hotel bed with Georgie.

His phone rang, and he pulled it out of his pocket, ready to switch it to silent. He definitely wasn't in the mood to talk to anyone. But a quick glance at the display showed King's number.

Better to get this over with now.

"Hey man. I figured you'd be calling. Georgie is at the Fitz-Simmons in a suite that I booked under my name. When I left she said she was going to bed."

"Good. I've been going crazy over here. Thanks for taking care of her." King sounded stressed as hell.

Truthfully, Jamie couldn't blame him for being stressed. A

Kingsley wedding was a huge social event and something people would be talking about for weeks even if it had gone off without a hitch. But to have a runaway bride *and* groom, it was the kind of thing that would feed the rumor mill for months. King was no doubt dealing with his parents and damage control with the media.

"Of course. No thanks needed."

"Still, I appreciate it. I know dealing with hysterical women is not exactly your favorite thing."

Jamie was suddenly grateful the conversation was taking place over the phone and not in person. There would be no way to hide his reaction. The last person he wanted to guess just how happy he'd been to be there for Georgie was her overprotective brother.

"How is she really? I just got off the phone with her, but she wasn't giving me anything."

Jamie was glad she'd kept her word and contacted her brother. It was clear that King's dominating personality was a struggle for Georgie to deal with. That made him smile. Despite what her brother thought, Georgie was just as strong-minded. She just didn't feel the need to assert her opinions at top volume.

"Good. I told her to call you so you wouldn't worry about her."

King grunted. "I'm going to worry anyway but at least she's already at the hotel. The vultures won't be able to find her as long as she's behind closed doors. The staff at the Fitz is loyal. Or at least they have been in the past."

Jamie gripped the phone tighter. The thought of Georgie having to fight off the press in the midst of everything made him feel completely helpless. The media barely bothered with him. Although he worked closely with the Kingsleys, he didn't have a famous last name or a bunch of extremely photogenic relatives for them to splash on the front page. He'd have to do something pretty crazy for the paparazzi to give a shit.

Something like steal Georgina Kingsley from her own wedding?

Jesus.

"So, anything we need to worry about?"

King was quiet. "It's bad, James. They're reporting that Alex had a mistress. And since he still can't be found either, they're saying he's run off to be with this mystery woman and abandoned Georgie. At least there are no pictures yet."

He sagged with relief and then immediately felt like an ass.

There were no pictures of him spiriting the bride away from the wedding, but the stories so far were bad enough. Georgie definitely wouldn't like being portrayed as the woman scorned.

Especially when that wasn't how things had gone down at all.

"I'll check on her first thing tomorrow. Make sure no one is bothering her."

"Wait, tomorrow? I thought you were going out of town?"

There was an uncomfortable pause before King cleared his throat. "James? Is everything okay?"

"Yeah. I figured I can swing by the hotel before I leave tomorrow morning. No big deal."

"Right." The way King dragged the word out made it clear that he wasn't buying it. "Just watch it."

Jamie ran a hand over his face, cutting off anything he might have said in the heat of the moment. Nothing that he would let fly right then would have been a productive comment to the man he thought of like a brother. Because all he really wanted was to tell King to fuck off and let him deal with Georgie.

"Glad to hear you have so much trust in me."

"That's not what I meant—"

"Look, I need to finish packing. Since my plans for tonight fell through, I'm going to use the time to go see my folks."

King hesitated before speaking again. "Cool. Tell everyone I said hi."

"Will do." Then he hung up and headed for his bedroom. Packing wasn't what he wanted to do but it was at least productive.

————

*T*he next morning, Georgie woke up to blinding sunlight. Groggy, she sat up and pushed her hair out of her face. It was tangled around her head like a rat's nest. She usually braided it or put it in a bun before bed.

Which meant that she hadn't washed her face before going to bed either. She turned her head slightly.

Yeah, black streaks all over the white pillowcase. House-keeping was going to love her.

"Great." She stood gingerly, ignoring the fuzzy, old socks taste in her mouth. Hangovers were just lovely, weren't they?

When things were all going to shit and a person needed a little liquid fortification, they shouldn't have to pay the price with a headache and garbage breath the next morning.

Really, that was just like kicking someone when they were down.

Georgie figured that this was about as down as she'd been in a long time. Or ever.

Ruined wedding. Sexual Rejection. Hangover. Bad Hair.

Yeah, things definitely weren't going her way lately. Then she stepped in front of the mirror, and a startled shriek erupted.

"Oh, dear God." She peered at her reflection in horror. There were not only black streaks all over her face from her mascara, but her eyelashes looked like they were glued together on one side forcing that eye wide open. It gave her a look of perpetual surprise. Combined with all the tangles on her head, she looked like she'd just been electrocuted.

"Suddenly really happy that Jamie turned me down now." It did give her a bit of a laugh to imagine his reaction if he'd woken up to this.

She headed into the bathroom and started the shower. This was going to require a head-to-toe scrub down.

Half an hour later, Georgie emerged from the bathroom scrubbed, brushed, polished and detangled. She was in the middle of towel drying her hair when her phone beeped.

It took her a minute to find it. King had couriered over some of her stuff last night, including her handbag and the suitcase from her bedroom that she'd packed for the honeymoon.

Georgie sighed. Knowing Alex, he was on their flight to Fiji right at that very moment. The look on his face when he'd realized she'd overheard him had been shocked but not devastated. It was unlikely that he was sitting in a hotel room alone feeling sorry for himself. She squared her shoulders and pushed more stuff out of the way until she found her phone.

Yesterday had been awful, but in the grand scheme of things she was lucky. And grateful. It might have taken her three years to see through Alex's games, but at least she'd found out. Some people lived their whole lives without knowing they were being used.

Her phone beeped again, and she blinked at all the little red flags visible.

She scrolled through her texts quickly. One was from Regina. It was dated early enough that it was probably when they'd first discovered her missing at the wedding.

Delete.

A few from wedding vendors. She rolled her eyes. Probably reminding her that she wasn't getting any money back.

Those could wait.

There were thirty voicemails on her phone. Georgie shook her head when she saw that about twenty of them were from her mother. That was something else she'd have to do today. Call her mother and listen to the barely concealed disappointment.

That could *definitely* wait.

But as she scrolled up, there was one from a number she didn't recognize that had come in just a few hours ago. Who would be calling her in the early morning? She clicked it and let the message play. Then almost dropped the phone when Alex's voice came through.

I'm so sorry, Georgie. This is not how I wanted you to find out.

There was some static, and then it sounded like he fumbled the phone. Was he drunk?

Can explain everything. Don't believe them. I know we can work this out.

The message cut off there. Georgie played it again, but it still didn't make much sense. What did he mean about not wanting her to find out? Did he really think that was the way to win her back, promising that he'd never wanted her to know he was just in it for the business contacts?

Not exactly the best apology.

And what was he saying about don't believe them? Believe who? She put her phone on the nightstand and sat on the edge of the bed. Clearly she wasn't the only one who'd been hitting the liquor the night before. Alex had apparently been drowning his sorrows at the bar, too. Although she wasn't sure why he was so depressed. Surely, he could find another heiress to dupe into marriage.

But it wouldn't be Georgina Kingsley. Never again.

Alex might have ruined her wedding day and Jamie might have rejected her last night, but she wasn't going down without a fight. She was determined to get her sexy on and she knew just where to do it.

She did still have her access key for Club VIP after all.

Chapter 6

*A*s he walked down the hallway, Jamie counted off the numbers as he passed. In order to avoid too much attention, he'd been sure to book Georgie a regular suite instead of one of the deluxe suites or the penthouse. Now he was wondering if that had been a bad move.

What kind of security was there on these regular floors? There was no one manning the elevator, so what was there to stop anyone from approaching her room?

He'd worked himself into a near frenzy by the time he reached her door. There was a room service tray right outside and the do-not-disturb sign was on the door. The faint sounds of the television were audible. He pulled out his phone and texted her.

Jamie: Knock. Knock.

Georgie: Um, who's there?

Jamie: Me. Right outside your hotel room. And did you really throw away a whole slice of key lime pie?

The door suddenly flew open and Georgie grabbed him by the front of the shirt. He allowed her to tug him inside.

"What are you doing outside my door, you weirdo? And stop staring at my leftovers!"

Jamie closed the door behind them and put the chain on. "I was just surprised you didn't eat that. I thought you had a sweet tooth."

Georgie shrugged but her cheeks went bright red. "I do have a sweet tooth. But it turns out key lime isn't my favorite anymore if I have it with breakfast, lunch and dinner."

She was so damn cute that he couldn't resist pulling her into a hug. That was when he noticed what she was wearing. A short black skirt and a sheer blouse that allowed a tantalizing amount of skin to peek through. Her hair had been styled in soft ringlets, and she was wearing that same dramatic makeup that made the color of her eyes look like a clear sky.

"You're dressed up. Were you going out?"

She was suddenly very interested in the paint color of her nails. "I was thinking about it. Why?"

He took the opportunity to move past her and examine the room. It looked like organized chaos with piles of clothes on the desk and chair, and then a bunch of lacy things on the bed. As he walked closer, he could feel his blood pressure rising. Were those...

"Thongs? You're trying on thongs?" he practically shouted.

Georgie rushed past him and snatched the offending lace off the comforter before stuffing them behind the pillow.

"That is private. Why did you come by, anyway? Wanted the opportunity to knock my self-esteem down another peg? More of the *it's not you, it's me* crap? Except it clearly is about me, since I'm the one who can't get laid!"

Her running commentary almost made him laugh until he looked around the room again and put the clues together.

Hot outfit.

Dramatic makeup.

Sexy underwear.

"You're not going back to that damn sex club!"

Georgie slapped a hand over his mouth. "Would you pipe down? I don't need everybody here knowing my business."

He pointed to the pillow hiding the thong collection. "You

don't think they'll find out when they see you walking through the lobby looking like sex on legs?"

"First, I'm not entirely sure what that even means. Second, contrary to some beliefs, thongs are usually not worn on the outside of your clothes. So no one would even see that."

"Except the guy you plan on showing them to, huh?"

She tilted her head as if considering it. As if actually considering it!

"You're not going back to that—"

Georgie spun around and poked one finger against his chest.

"I don't know who you think you are, but this is none of your business, Jamie."

"None of my business?"

All control gone, he scooped her up in his arms ignoring her screech of outrage. It took a bit of maneuvering, but finally, he had her spread out on the bed beneath him.

When he lowered down, settling gently between her legs, Georgie stopped thrashing.

"Jamie?"

"Hmm?" He was busy inhaling the scent of her hair. What was that fragrance she always carried around with her? It was like injecting liquid sex into his veins every time he got a whiff of it.

"You're hard. Again."

He chuckled. "That seems to be a regular problem around you."

She gulped. "You said you didn't want to do that."

"I definitely didn't say that. I probably said some bullshit about how it was a bad idea and I didn't want to hurt you. Which is still true. But I thought about what you said."

Her eyes swung to his. "You did?"

This close it was unexpectedly intimate. That sounded weird considering that he was on top of her practically dry humping, but Georgie had the kind of eyes that could see right through you. It made him acutely aware of just how much was at stake here.

"You were right. Life is short, and you should experience it all now. We can have one night without anyone being hurt. I'm leaving for a business trip soon anyway, so there won't be time for either of us to get attached."

"So, what are you saying?" Georgie's fingers tightened around his biceps as she waited for his answer.

"I'm saying that if you want to explore sex, I'd rather you do it with me."

Her lips twitched. "Like you're doing me a favor?"

"Hell, no. If anyone is doing the favor, it's you. You're offering a chance to explore this sexy as fuck body, and I'm just the lucky bastard who is coming along for the ride."

She nodded but there was a vulnerability in her eyes that made him hold her a little bit tighter. For all her big talk about sexual exploration, this was still Georgie. His perfect princess who had been sheltered all of her life. Maybe she really was ready to branch out, but what if she wasn't? It sounded insane to think he was volunteering to be her revenge fuck to keep her out of trouble, but he sure as hell didn't want her asking anyone else.

"Let's go slow and see what happens. Work for you?"

Her grin made him feel about ten feet tall. "Yeah, that works for me."

"Okay, well let's find a movie on demand and see about getting some food."

It was going to kill him to take it slow, but if that was what Georgie needed, then he needed to find something to distract them. Fast.

*A*s he rolled over and sat up, Georgie could confess to being just the tiniest bit confused.

First he'd barged in, making demands and being his usual annoying self. But then he'd suddenly turned all seductive and had her flat on her back before she could blink. She thought agreeing to be her revenge sex partner was a good thing.

But no, Jamie was sitting back on the bed and changing the channels on the TV like he was ready for a movie marathon. His moods seemed to change on a dime sometimes, and she wasn't sure she could keep up.

Where was the passion? Shouldn't they be ripping each other's clothes off now?

Georgie thought back to all the times she'd waited for Alex to initiate things. All those years she'd hoped maybe he'd try something new or show any interest in finding out what *she* wanted.

Well, she was done waiting. If she wanted something done, she was going to have to make it happen. Starting now.

Her hands trembled only slightly as she unbuttoned her blouse to reveal the black bra underneath.

Jamie looked over at her. "What should we watch... Whoa. Georgie, what are you doing?"

It was hard not to laugh at the instantly befuddled look on his face. He looked like a little kid staring at a toy he desperately wanted but had been told not to touch.

"Getting more comfortable. Isn't that what you said?" She toyed with the straps of the bra, but just when she thought his tongue was going to fall out, she started unzipping her skirt instead.

"Uh, maybe we should..." He never finished the thought just stared at her legs as she pushed the skirt down. "Fucking hell, Georgie. You are beautiful."

The simple reverence in his voice was what gave her the confidence to unhook her bra in the back. It hung on her arms for a few seconds and she clutched it to her chest before it could fall away, revealing her bare breasts to him.

"Show me." The gruff tone wasn't at all what she was used to hearing from Jamie. But the stark need and desire sparked something that made her want to do it. With him she wanted to be bad.

Because she knew he would make her feel so good.

She straightened her arms and the bra fell to the ground, leaving her clad in only a black lace thong.

"You take my breath away."

That was the last thing he said before he yanked her against him. Georgie grabbed his arms, climbing him like a tree. For the next few moments, they broke apart only to get him out of his clothes, his shirt, jeans and then boxers being pushed down and thrown in a frenzy.

When Georgie got her first look at him naked, she wasn't sure if she should give herself a high five or run away and barricade herself in the bathroom. The man was not built like someone who spent his time behind a desk.

Jamie had the kind of body that looked like he knew how to use it. Like he had the stamina to give her the ride of her life. She could only hope she was ready to handle that. After so long with one person, she really had no idea what men expected from their sexual partners.

What if he wanted her to do things she couldn't handle? Or things that hurt?

His tongue lashed against the sensitive shell of her ear. "Don't worry. I'll go easy on you."

His chuckle made her feel better. Ultimately, this was still Jamie, which made all the difference. With him, she didn't have to wonder if he liked her body or thought she was pretty. Even the way he looked at her was different.

As if he could hear her thoughts, Jamie tugged her gently to the bed, going to his knee beside her.

"If anything is uncomfortable, let me know."

"Okay."

"If anything feels good, let me know that, too." He raised an eyebrow at her soft giggle. "Totally serious about that. I want to know what works for you so I can do it again and again."

Her thoughts scattered as he dipped his head and his lips met the skin right above her panties. His thumb hooked in the side of the fabric and tugged it down, his mouth following close behind. She had no time to prepare before his mouth connected with her bare skin.

The sound she made would have embarrassed her if she had time to care, but Jamie was clearly on a mission. Then he looked up at her, and the intensity of his eyes while he was kissing her so intimately was all it took to make her fly apart.

"Fuck, I knew you were hot, but watching you come is the sexiest thing I've ever seen."

Georgie was still tingling all over, and his words barely got through the post-orgasmic haze she was caught in. She'd had orgasms before, after all she did own a vibrator, but they were nothing like what had just happened. There were so many sensations that couldn't be replicated when going solo. The warm, wet rasp of his tongue, the weight of his arms around her and holding her down, and mostly, the deliciously dirty things he loved to say.

This time when he kissed her, it was hard and unrelenting, and his lips tasted like her. It was an unexpected turn on and made her feel strangely possessive. Like he should smell and taste like her and only her.

"Are you sure about this, Georgie?" His dark eyes fixed on hers, and there was something there that she couldn't define. But all she knew was that she'd never seen that particular look from Jamie and that she never wanted to lose it.

"I want you. I want this." Her hand snaked down and wrapped around him.

He growled, the sound low and sexy, before he pulled back slightly. She watched as he reached for his pants and then blushed when he withdrew a condom. How crazy he made her! She'd forgotten all about protection.

As if he could hear her thoughts, he smirked while rolling the condom on. She bit her lip as he crawled back across the mattress.

"Enjoying the show, princess?"

She raised an eyebrow. "Very much so. I'd enjoy it even more from up close."

This time when he kissed her, there was no uncertainty. All her thoughts were attuned to him and the way he made her feel. They fit perfectly together and when he thrust into her, her mouth fell open from the exquisite pleasure of being stretched full.

"Oh my God, Jamie."

Her fingers clutched at him until she was surely leaving marks on his skin. But his deep moan of satisfaction when their hips finally met made her shamelessly wet.

"I knew it. Knew you'd be perfect," he muttered, and the deep sound of his voice rumbling next to her ear made her shudder and clench around him.

He lifted one of her legs and held it around his waist to deepen the angle, and all Georgie could do was hang on as he proceeded to fuck her into the mattress. She moaned and trembled in his grip. Before long she was coming again, crying out as her muscles clamped down on him relentlessly.

She felt his smile against her neck as he slowed his pace. Pushing up on one hand, Jamie rested his forehead against hers. He kept their eyes locked as he made love to her until Georgie felt tears well.

"You are absolutely perfect." His voice broke off when she

tightened her muscles around him deliberately. "Fuck, do that again."

The ragged command made Georgie feel like the sexiest woman in the world. She tightened her muscles again, crying out when he fucked her harder, the move having stolen away whatever control was holding him back.

Yes, she thought. This was what she wanted. To have the unbridled, uncontrolled Jamie that had been haunting her dreams for years. Her eyes drifted closed.

"No, let me see you. Keep those beautiful eyes on me as you come."

Georgie gasped as he suddenly rolled over, placing her on top. She wasn't used to being in the driver's seat and immediately felt awkward. But Jamie placed her hands on his chest and rolled his hips.

"Ride me, Georgie. Take what you need."

Under his hot stare, she felt like she could do anything and it would turn him on. Once she caught his rhythm, she rocked her hips, taking him deeper. His eyes bounced between her breasts and down to where they were joined. The look on his face was pure rapture.

And pure adoration.

"Christ, I'm going to come. Come with me." Jamie licked his thumb and then held it right against her clit, rubbing furiously.

Georgie screamed as the orgasm rolled over her unexpectedly. Dimly, she heard his hoarse groan that proved he'd finished right behind her. She collapsed against his chest and curled up, feeling completely satisfied.

Chapter 7

*O*f all the things that Jamie had worried about happening in the aftermath of sex with Georgie, he'd certainly never prepared himself for laughter.

"Should I be worried that you can't seem to stop giggling to yourself?"

Georgie snuggled down lower under the comforter, peeking out at him from under the curtain of her hair. "Don't mind me, I'm just delirious from multiple orgasms."

Jamie found himself chuckling along when she let loose another satisfied hum. "Glad to know you found the service satisfactory. Be sure to fill out a quality control survey before you leave."

She rolled over until she was flat on her back. Her smile was gone. "I never had this with..."

He scowled. "It's okay. You can say his name. Alex the Asshole."

"The funny thing is his middle name is Aaron so his initials were a tad too close to spelling out ass for my liking. Anyway, we never had this."

"What is this?" Suddenly Jamie wanted to hear her describe it. He wanted her take on this thing between them because it suddenly didn't feel like the easy, fun fling that they'd planned.

"I don't know," she replied, finally.

Jamie propped himself up on one elbow. "This is what happens when two people have insane chemistry. It's natural. Then there's the fact that it's you and me. It's not like we're strangers. We already care about each other, so it's easier to lose your inhibitions with someone when you know they like you just the way you are."

She was watching him closely now. "You liked me? Even when I was following you around and insulting you?"

"Flinging insults is another type of foreplay. At least it is for us." The clock on the nightstand caught his eye. "Damn, is that the time?"

Georgie stiffened and then pushed away slightly. "Yeah, I guess you have to get going. I can walk you out."

"You can't leave!"

She froze, her hands clutching the comforter to her chest. "What? Why can't I leave?"

"Um, shit."

"Jamie, what are you keeping from me?"

"I hate to even bring it up, but the gossip rags are reporting that Alex had a mistress. It's probably best to lay low for a while."

She nodded but her eyes had dimmed a bit. He hated to see that look on her face and even more that he'd been the one to bring it back. But at least he knew one way to get rid of it again.

He grabbed the edge of the comforter and yanked it down until her bare breasts popped free.

"Jamie! What the hell?"

"I like you better uncovered."

She tugged her end of the comforter again. "Maybe so, but I need to get dressed."

"Why? All I'm going to do is get you undressed all over again."

Her eyes heated at his words.

"You didn't think I was leaving, did you?" He chuckled darkly. "Oh, my sweet, innocent Georgie. You really have no idea what you've started, do you?"

He climbed over her again. "A revenge fuck doesn't mean just one time, beautiful."

"It doesn't?" She moaned as his hand moved up to cup one breast, his fingers skimming over the sensitive tip.

"Not a chance. I have the opportunity to do all the things I've dreamed about with you, and you'll be lucky if I let you sleep tonight."

"Mmm. All night, huh?"

The hint of challenge in her voice was unmistakable. "You don't think I can do it?"

Her eyes sparkled. "That's a long time, that's all."

"You're right. Seeing is believing."

———

*E*xhausted after their second round, Georgie watched as Jamie paced the room. He wasn't wearing a stitch, not even a towel, and he had the room service menu in one hand and the television remote in the other.

It should have been an inconvenience. After all, he'd barged in and taken over her bed and her remote. This was supposed to be her time to reflect on her mistakes so she could hopefully never make them again.

But instead she was holed up with Jamie playing naked games.

She really liked naked games.

"Hamburger or pasta?" Jamie waved the menu in the air and she had the feeling he'd been trying to get her attention for a bit.

"I already ate lunch, remember? But I'm not against eating again."

Now that she had no more worries about fitting into her wedding dress, she could actually eat to enjoy food again. She groaned thinking about the slice of key lime pie she'd already wasted.

"On second thought, nothing for me. I'll just steal a fry from your plate."

Jamie grinned. "Two orders of fries. I speak girl. Steal a fry is code for eat half of the plate."

After he put in the order, he climbed back under the covers next to her. Georgie slid over and cuddled up right below his chin. This was the most unexpected part. The snuggling. Feeling so safe. Happy.

This was supposed to be a casual thing. A revenge fuck to get her over Alex and show her how good sex could be.

She peeked up at Jamie, whose attention was still on the television. So far, not only had he blown all thoughts of her former fiancé out of her mind, but he'd been so sweet and attentive. It was enough to make any girl feel a little obsessed.

No. Not happening. Georgie, you are not doing this again. You kicked the Jamie crush a long time ago.

She pulled the comforter higher to ward off the sudden chill. Her crush on Jamie had died the day he'd brushed her off. Now that she was older, she could understand his point of view better. He'd been a twenty-two-year-old visiting his best friend's family. She'd been a completely naïve sixteen-year-old who didn't see a single thing wrong with throwing herself into his arms.

In retrospect, she actually thought he'd done a pretty good job of turning her down without humiliating her. But teenage Georgie hadn't cared about how nice he was being. All she'd remembered was that he'd said no and that she'd seen him with a busty blonde later that same day.

"What are you thinking about?" Jamie's voice interrupted her thoughts.

She contemplated making something up but then decided, why bother? They were both older and wiser. Plus, considering where they were, it was kind of funny.

"I was thinking about my sweet sixteen party. When you crushed my teenage heart."

Jamie groaned and put a hand over his face. "You had to bring that up, didn't you?"

She laughed. "It's pretty relevant, considering what we just did."

"Do you have any idea what a pervert I felt like that day?"

"Why? Because I kissed you? We're not that far apart in age."

"No. But six years is a big deal when one of you is *jailbait*." He glared down at her. "You were literally a walking felony. Why do you think I stopped coming around after that? Every time I saw you, I was reminded of how many ways King would dismember my body if I so much as breathed in your direction."

"Well, teenage Georgie had some pretty damn good taste." She bit her lip, wondering whether she should tell him the next part. "You're the reason I waited, you know? I didn't want my first time to be with just anyone. I kept thinking that maybe when I was older, you'd finally see me as a woman."

His eyes locked onto hers. "I did. That was why I had to stay away. I didn't trust myself then. Hell, I don't trust myself with you now."

"You should. I've never felt the way I do with you. That's probably the thing I'll regret the most once this all sinks in. If things had been different, my first time could have been with you and none of this would have happened."

Immediately, she clamped her lips shut. Her blabbermouth was always getting her into trouble. This was supposed to be a fun, casual encounter, and here she was vomiting up all her fears and regrets. Jamie hadn't been planning on leaving, but he probably would want to soon if she didn't shut up. But when she looked up, he didn't appear upset by her outburst at all.

"Georgie, you don't need to have any regrets. Alex may have been your first, but there's no special talent to being first.

Whatever man wins your heart will be last. And that's all that matters."

Moved more than she could express, Georgie pulled him closer and kissed him. What started out as a tender expression of her feelings soon spiraled out of control as she climbed on top of him, grinding against his lap.

Jamie groaned suddenly. "I really hate to be a buzzkill, but we have to stop."

"What? Why?"

"Because I wasn't exactly planning on this when I came over. So I didn't bring enough protection, just the two that were in my wallet."

Grinning, Georgie climbed down and rushed over to her suitcase. "Lucky for us, I'm a packrat." She unzipped the case and rested it gently on its side. Then she reached beneath the neatly layered clothes for the box of condoms she'd packed.

Jamie shook his head at her. "Prepared for anything. One of the things I love about you."

Her head snapped up and she fought to keep the surprise off her face. It was a casual comment and the kind of thing he probably said to women all the time without realizing its effect. She wasn't silly enough to think he actually meant it.

But there was no denying the little burst of pleasure she'd felt hearing those words from him. Which was something she had to cut off right then and there.

After tonight, Jamie would go back to his place, and she'd go back to her room at her parents' house. This was a sexy, secret moment hidden in time that would never be spoken of and never repeated. The only thing that could ruin it was if she started attaching emotions to it.

So she'd do what she promised and indulge in a wicked sex marathon before going back to her prim and proper life.

What happened in that hotel room would stay in that hotel room.

Life was short, and she was living in the moment. And there was no one she'd rather do that with than Jamie.

As long as she remembered their deal.

Revenge sex only.

Emotions. Never.

"Yeah, I'm prepared, but this box has six in here so we won't need all of these."

When she got close to the bed, Jamie reached out and tugged her down. "Hell yes, we will. But don't worry. If we run out, there are a few other things I can show you."

Chapter 8

*I*t was the middle of the night, and Georgie was cuddled up to his side. He should've been sleeping. But all he could do was watch her. They had so little time left together, and he knew this would have to be enough.

She murmured in her sleep, and he couldn't resist trailing a finger over her soft cheek.

It felt so right. The last time he'd felt this safe was when he was a child before his father left for the first time. Back then he'd known his parents were unhappy and fought a lot, however, it had never occurred to him that he'd wake up one morning and his father would be gone. They were a family, and families belonged together. That was what his mother always said.

It wasn't until he was older that he understood she was saying it to convince herself as much as anyone else. Sometimes he still wondered how it had all gone so wrong.

His father hadn't come from a wealthy family, but his grandparents had done pretty well later in life. His grandfather had been a mechanic who owned his own garage. His grandmother had run the front office for years. Together they worked hard to maintain a solid upper middle-class life and tried to help their son.

His father, Jim Junior, didn't appreciate the help. Instead he spent all the money he earned working at the garage on card games, determined that his lucky break was just around the corner. When his career as a card shark didn't pan out, he'd started buying real estate courses from ads he saw on television.

By this time, Jamie was almost a teenager, and his bullshit meter had been finely honed even then. He'd hoped that his mother would be the voice of reason, but Helen Hamilton was firmly in his dad's corner. No matter what crazy scheme his father came up with, his mother was right there cheering him on.

Shockingly, his father hadn't become a millionaire from investing in real estate either. The only thing Jim Junior had a talent for was wasting money and making Jamie's mother cry.

When his grandparents passed away, they'd left the bulk of

their estate in a trust for Jamie that could only be accessed after he married. Then they'd left a small amount to his parents.

His parents' inheritance had been gone within a year.

Jamie was lucky the money for his education had been put into a separate special trust for him. If his parents had been able to access it, they would have spent that, too.

It was a sobering thing to realize your parents weren't who you thought they were. But as he'd gotten older and more successful it had become clear they only cared about two things.

Their ongoing feud.

And money.

Now that Jamie had money of his own, they were interested in him. Or at least, they were interested only as long as it took for him to write them another check. Then they were off doing whatever new scheme they'd cooked up. It would have been funny if it wasn't so sad.

It didn't bother him the way it used to. He'd long ago accepted them for who they were. They could no more change their stripes than a lion could change into a lamb.

But that didn't mean it had no effect on him. Maybe that was why he'd bonded with King so hard and fast.

They'd met in college and had so much in common. But it was the way King had talked about his family that drew him in. It was everything Jamie had always wanted and been denied. Two parents who loved and respected each other. Siblings who actually cared if he came home for holidays and summer break.

Somehow King had known what Jamie needed and insisted that he come home with him whenever possible. In many ways, their friendship had saved him. King was the first person who saw who he really was and liked him anyway.

Georgie was the first person who made him want to be better.

"I wish I could be the guy for you, princess. But I don't know how to be what you need. My parents have been together off and on for thirty years, and all they do is fight. Break up and then make up. That's not what I want for you."

But he could pretend for one night. Here in the darkness, he could close his eyes and imagine a world where Georgie was his and he was the lucky man who'd earned her love. Every morning he'd wake up excited to see her and every night he'd be reluctant to go to sleep because he wanted more time.

For a few glimmering moments, he believed it could actually happen. He'd stop working sixteen-hour days. King would kick his ass once and then they'd shake on it and be brothers legally as well as in spirit. And he'd have Georgie, smiling at him in that way only she could. The one that made him believe he was worthy.

But like all dreams, it only made sense in the dark. In the light of day, Georgie wouldn't want a workaholic playboy with feuding spendthrift parents. He had nothing to offer her but problems. She was just out of one bad situation. She deserved a chance to shine.

"One day you'll find the guy. The one who'll be your last and I'll smile and pretend like I'm happy for you. But inside I'll be wishing it could be me."

Georgie sighed in her sleep, and he waited to see if she would wake. When her breathing evened out, he curled up closer and put his arm around her. Just like every other time he touched her, she moved closer, seeking his touch. Even asleep she trusted him.

It wasn't the dream, but it was enough.

It would have to be.

---

*F*or the second time, Georgie woke to blinding sunlight in her face. She'd forgotten to close the curtains again. But this time, she just smiled.

Then she rolled over and looked at Jamie.

He was on his back with one arm thrown over his head. Immediately, she remembered his whispered confessions the night before. She wished she could reach out and brush a hand over the dirty blond hair flopping on his forehead, but that would wake him up and she wasn't ready for that yet. He didn't know that she'd been awake, and she wasn't sure if he would react negatively knowing she'd heard all that.

It was a shock to her that his family life was so rough. It was something that she'd never have guessed since King had never mentioned it and Jamie always seemed like he had everything together.

It made her like him even more, knowing that he'd achieved so much despite an unhappy home life. And it made her wish for things she had no right to. Like that she could be the woman who showed him what unconditional love was.

Only that wasn't their agreement. That wasn't what Jamie wanted.

But until he woke up, their night together wasn't over yet.

And she wouldn't have to face the reality that one night with Jamie hadn't been nearly enough.

"I can feel you staring at me," he grumbled, before opening one eye.

"Sorry. The sun woke me up." Georgie sat up and self-consciously ran her fingers through her hair trying to arrange it in some semblance of normalcy. The memory of how she'd looked yesterday morning had her climbing out of bed and going straight to the bathroom. Luckily she didn't look bad today. Even though her hair was wild, her cheeks had a rosy hue and her skin had a certain glow.

She looked like a woman who'd spent all night having spectacular sex.

"Morning. Why'd you run off?" Jamie appeared in the mirror behind her before burying his face in the crook of her neck.

"I didn't want to kiss you with morning breath."

He scoffed. "Who cares about that?"

When his arms tightened around her waist, Georgie grabbed her toothbrush from the sink and stuck it in her mouth.

Jamie cracked up. "You think that'll stop me?"

She nodded. "I hope so."

"You're such a goof. Go ahead. I'll brush too. Then we can be minty fresh together."

He opened one of the complimentary toothbrushes provided by the hotel and then reached for the toothpaste. She held out her brush and he put some paste on hers first and then his. They stood at the mirror brushing their teeth until she started giggling.

"This is weird," she said around a mouthful of paste.

He spat in the sink and rinsed his mouth out, waiting for her to do the same. "What's so weird about it?"

She shrugged. "I'm so used to seeing you in suits. Always perfect. Always businesslike. Now everything is different."

He picked her up and then set her on the counter. "It is. Now you know my secret. I'm not perfect. I have morning breath, and I always wake up horny." He kissed her lightly.

She laughed against his mouth.

"But seriously, I'm glad I got to see this other side of you. Last night, it was about more than just revenge sex for me. You're pretty amazing, you know that?"

He looked bashful. "I do all right."

"I'm being serious. I really want to thank you."

Now he just looked annoyed. "You don't have to thank me, Georgie. It wasn't exactly hard work on my part."

She winked. "Well, it felt pretty hard to me."

"Nice. Now I have you making dirty jokes. My work here is done."

"I wasn't thanking you for the orgasms, by the way. I was talking about the part that came before the sex. Now I know what I was missing."

Suddenly he looked uncomfortable. "I was just doing what any guy should do. You are a beautiful, strong, sweet woman. You should be fucking worshipped."

He didn't say anything else and Georgie suddenly had the urge to cry. Especially after what she'd overheard the prior night, she understood what he wasn't saying. He truly believed she deserved to be treated like a queen.

But he wasn't the guy who would do that.

Their time was up.

"Thank you, Jamie. For everything."

She ignored his questioning look. Even though she understood where he was coming from and why, it was still going to be hard to accept that this was as far as he was willing to go.

He could talk about all the things she deserved but he couldn't give them to her. It was fair, but it still sucked.

"At least now I know what to look for in the next guy. The right guy." She hopped down from the counter, avoiding his eyes.

"Yeah, the right guy," Jamie repeated.

They cleaned up the suite together, Jamie watching her pack her suitcase without comment. So many times Georgie wanted to stop and yell at him or even throw one of the black thongs he'd complained about at his head.

But in the end, he was doing the sensible thing. The right thing. And she couldn't hate him for that.

He called for a bellboy to come get her suitcase, and then they walked together to the elevator.

"I'll go down first just in case there are any photographers who have figured out you're here. King said the staff here is loyal, but I figure it's worth checking."

Georgie clutched at the strap of her handbag. Was this really how they were going to leave things? With a polite goodbye in the hotel hallway?

He must have read the hurt in her expression because he

whispered, "Princess." The amount of emotion in that one word almost made her bawl her eyes out.

"I'm fine. I will be fine. We had a damn good time and now I have to go back and deal with my life. This time next week, it'll be like this never happened."

When he didn't look convinced, Georgie stuck out her hand. He ignored it and pulled her into a hug, and she took a final moment to memorize his scent and the feel of his arms around her. Because the only way she could uphold her promise to keep things casual was to avoid him completely. So this was the last hit of the Jamie drug that she'd be getting for a long time.

Finally she pulled back and plastered on a big, fake grin. "See, I told you we could go back to normal. You go back to acting like a robot, and I'll insult you every chance I get. Okay, asshole?"

It took a long time, but he finally smiled. "Back to normal."

Chapter 9

The next week was busy, and Jamie was grateful for the distraction. When Georgie had promised they'd go back to hating each other, he'd thought she was kidding.

But every time he saw her now, she was just as sarcastic and dismissive as she'd ever been. Instead of looking up at him with those sparkling blue eyes, she looked through him like he wasn't even there. There were no more hugs or opportunities to touch her, not even in the most casual of ways. She stayed on the opposite side of the room like he was a stranger.

Like he was an enemy.

When they'd agreed to go back to hating each other, he hadn't thought she'd meant to treat him like a stranger. Where were his sweet smiles? The little glances he'd gotten used to but hadn't missed until they were gone?

He never thought he'd say he regretted a night of hot sex, but part of him wondered if that night hadn't ruined things between them. Because the little bit of Georgie he'd been getting before was better than this barren wasteland.

"Don't forget the Europe trip is coming up soon. I assume you're going to put in for it again this year?" King asked before taking another sip of his drink.

They were at *Les Printemps*, a fancy French restaurant in D.C. It was one of the main spots Kingsley International used to wine and dine clients. They'd just finished up a client meeting.

"I already did. Unless you want it this year?"

King gave him an incredulous look. "Six weeks away from home? No, thank you."

Jamie smirked. "Quite a change from a year ago. I thought I would have to fight you for that assignment last year."

King shrugged. "I didn't have any reason to stay home last year."

The words hit home. Jamie loved going to Europe. Usually he

did, anyway. It was an opportunity to take a company-paid vacation and all he had to do was woo clients and potential investors in a few different countries. It was an opportunity only offered to senior executives, but lately more of them had declined due to family obligations. Jamie had always thought it was a win for him and for King, who also loved to travel.

Now it looked like he would have prime pick of all travel opportunities. Why did that make him feel so lonely?

"Well, I'll be sure to enjoy the trip on your behalf."

King grinned. "It'll be fun. Maybe Olivia and I will meet you in Paris while you're there. I haven't taken her on a vacation yet."

"I'm sure she would love that." Jamie paused with his drink at his lips. At a table behind them a group of women were laughing loudly. One of the laughs was incredibly familiar. Then the woman turned her head toward him. "Is that Georgie?"

King turned in his seat. "Hey, I think it is. We should go say hello."

"No, I'm sure she's busy. It looks like she's with friends."

"Probably. That asshole Alex apparently didn't like her to go out with her friends, so she mentioned wanting to make up for lost time." King held up a finger and their waiter appeared a few moments later.

While his friend paid the bill, Jamie's eyes kept going back to Georgie. She looked happy. Her dark hair was twisted up into some kind of complicated knot and she was wearing a pink sweater that made her eyes look even bluer. As they approached her table, the huge smile on her face disappeared.

There was a flirtatious chorus of hellos as several of the other women at the table waved at them.

Georgie rolled her eyes. "King. Jamie. What are you doing here?"

"Dinner with clients. And actually, I have to go. Olivia just called me, which means I'm late for something. Good to see you, sis." King gave Jamie a quick wave as he left, his phone already glued to his ear.

"And he's off. I haven't seen him move that fast since college," Jamie remarked.

"Neither have I," one of the women at the table replied making the rest of them laugh.

"Or maybe he just loves his girlfriend. Something you wouldn't understand." Georgie's eyes might as well have been daggers.

"He does." Jamie tried to hold her gaze, but she turned to the woman next to her, dismissing him.

What the hell?

This time last week, she'd had her tongue in his mouth, but now she couldn't bother with a conversation? When they'd first met, Georgie had been super sweet to him. There hadn't been any bad blood between them until that damned sweet sixteen party. King liked to joke that the two of them were like oil and water. They naturally didn't mix. But that was because King didn't remember that it hadn't always been this way between them.

He had proof that Georgie liked him just fine when the lights were out.

Fuming, Jamie walked over to the bar. He slid a handful of bills across the polished wooden surface.

"I want you to send a round of drinks to the table in the corner. Where the woman in the pink sweater is currently sitting. Then another round ten minutes after that."

The bartender nodded. "Got it."

Jamie pulled out his phone as he walked to the back of the restaurant where the bathrooms were located.

As soon as Georgie answered, he said, "Tell the girls you have to go to the bathroom, otherwise, I'm coming back and we'll talk in front of them. Your choice."

———

*I*t took a few minutes, but Georgie finally appeared in the hallway behind him. "Why are you still here? I thought you left after King did. And why did our table just get a massive drink order out of nowhere?"

He grabbed her hand and pulled her into the ladies' room, flicking the lock after they were inside. Georgie watched him warily. Even when she was snarking at him, it was still better than being ignored.

"I'm here because you've been treating me like I have a communicable disease ever since last week. What's up with that?"

She wouldn't meet his eyes. "I thought that was what you wanted. You said we had to go back to normal."

"Normal isn't pretending we don't know each other, Georgie." With every word he got closer. Her eyelids fluttered slightly as he moved into her personal space.

Just like that, he calmed. Jamie shook his head. Apparently all he'd needed to cure his foul mood this week was this. To see Georgie. To have her sweet scent wrap around him.

Georgie didn't seem like she was getting quite the same satisfaction. Her eyes flashed up at him as she snapped, "Well, it seemed like that was the way you wanted it. You didn't even have time to call me afterward to make sure I got home."

He'd never heard her voice sound so small. Jamie could have kicked himself. He'd been so determined to play things cool and keep it casual, that he'd hurt her unintentionally.

"If you think I just went back to work like nothing happened, that's not true. I've been sporting this all week." He pressed closer so she could feel the hard length at the front of his pants.

Georgie bit her lip. "That feels uncomfortable."

"Tell me about it. Not the most convenient thing when in a meeting with ten other dudes either."

She laughed softly. "I bet. Sucks to be you, huh?"

"Right now, no one is sucking on anything. Which is a shame."

Georgie pinched him. "Is there a point to this?"

"I have to go to Europe for company business soon, but there's no reason we can't have a little fun until then."

The more Jamie thought about it, the more sense it made. Since he had to leave soon, it was like a natural break point.

There was no risk of hurt feelings when things were so clearly defined ahead of time.

"A little fun?" Georgie tilted her head. "More fun like that thing you did in the hotel room?"

"Thing? What do you mean?" He almost laughed out loud at the frustrated expression on her face. God, he loved messing with her. She was so much fun to tease.

She pinched his waist. "You know what I mean. That thing with your tongue that made me scream my head off."

"Oh, *that* thing. That could definitely be arranged. There's just one condition."

She sighed. "There's always a catch."

"It's not a big thing. Just that we have to also do this part."

When she wrinkled her nose in confusion, Jamie could feel the heat climbing from the neck of his shirt. Apparently he was going to have to spell it out.

"The part where you talk to me. Where we kiss. And you don't ignore me when I talk to you."

Her eyes softened. "You're a nice guy, Jamie Hamilton. Who would've guessed? But you're in luck because I like this part, too. Especially the part where I get to smell you." She buried her face in his neck and inhaled.

"You're so weird."

"I am. But you like it."

And that was the problem. He did.

This was the worst possible time for him to be carrying on a secret affair with the boss's daughter. Not only because it would look bad if it got out but also because it could ruin his career. He'd worked hard to earn an executive position next to King. It wasn't easy to do for someone outside of the family. He finally had everything he'd ever wanted; money, power and respect from people he admired.

His unrelenting obsession with Georgie could torpedo all of that in a heartbeat.

Too bad none of those very logical reasons were going to be enough to keep him away from her.

A loud knock at the door startled them both.

"*Oh my god,*" Georgie whispered. "*Someone's outside the door.* Um, just a minute!"

Jamie covered his mouth to keep from laughing and giving it away.

"This is not funny, Jamie. People know me here. I can't be seen sneaking out of the bathroom with a guy! Go hide in the stall. I'll leave first, and hopefully whoever it is won't know you were in here with me."

"Little problem. No, big problem. I still have this." He looked down at the huge erection that was incredibly obvious due to the cut of his trousers.

Georgie looked mortified. Then she bit her lip again. "So, what do you propose we do about that?"

"How about this?" He tipped up her chin and kissed her softly on the lips. He could tell it wasn't what she'd been expecting by the soft little "*oh*" she muttered right before she practically melted into his arms.

"Meet me at my place in an hour." He held his breath until she nodded.

"But I can't stay over," Georgie insisted. "If we're going to keep this secret, then I definitely can't be seen walking out of your building in the early morning."

He nodded before going to hide in a stall. A few seconds later, he heard a random voice, and then it was quiet. He waited another five minutes before he left.

If anyone had told him he'd be willing to hide out in a women's bathroom, he wouldn't have believed it. But there was something about Georgie that pushed him over the edge. He felt like an addict craving a fix. He wasn't sure what she'd done to him in that hotel room, but he wasn't going to be happy until he got another taste.

She was proving to be more of a distraction than he ever could have predicted. He was playing with fire and caring less and less every day about getting burned.

Chapter 10

*S*neaking around had never been her favorite thing. Even as a child, Georgie had always resisted the urge to peek at her Christmas presents out of fear of being caught.

Jamie didn't seem to mind the clandestine nature of their relationship at all. In fact, he'd proven to be a most inventive secret lover. He made her come at a movie theater with one hand up her skirt. He'd made love to her in the front seat of his Range Rover. She still wasn't sure how that had worked.

But as much fun as she was having with him, it all came with an unexpected consequence. Georgie shifted uneasily as she climbed carefully into the front seat of her car.

She'd been sore for the past two days from all the sex.

Hopefully they sold some kind of cream at the drugstore to help with intimate problems. It wasn't the kind of thing she could ask anyone about so if the aisles at the store weren't clearly labeled, she was screwed.

What do you think it'll say, Georgie? Cream for an overused va-jay-jay, Aisle 13?

She'd only been driving for about ten minutes when smoke started coming from beneath the hood of her car. Terrified, Georgie pulled on to the shoulder and called Jamie.

"Hey, princess. You're calling early tonight."

"Jamie, I think my car is on fire."

"Wait, what?"

"Okay not on fire but there's definitely smoke."

She could hear him moving around. "Are you somewhere safe?"

"Not really. I'm on 495." She peered at the exit a few yards down and told him what it said.

"Okay, is the car still smoking?"

"No, actually it looks like it stopped."

"In that case, stay in the car. You're safer inside than standing on the side of the road where you could get hit. I'll be right there."

Ten minutes later, Jamie pulled up behind her. Georgie immediately felt like everything was going to be all right. The situation completely proved Jamie's point about her being a sheltered princess, but she wasn't ready to examine that too closely. All she knew was that when something scary had happened, she'd immediately called Jamie.

Not her father.

Not King.

Jamie.

As she watched him approach the car on the passenger side, she decided she wasn't ready to examine that little revelation just yet either.

She rolled down the window. *"Hey sugar, you looking for a date?"*

He squinted at her.

Georgie rolled her eyes. "Seriously? It's from *Pretty Woman*."

His lips twitched. "Pop the hood for me. Do you know how to do that?"

"Of course, I do. I'm not completely helpless."

After he moved on, she frantically tried to remember the things her brother had insisted on showing her when she started driving. One day she was going to have to thank him for trying to make her as independent as possible. It often came off as condescending, but he really was doing it out of love. And he'd been right, as usual. She did need to know this stuff.

Not that she'd ever tell him that part.

It took long enough for Jamie to start making faces at her through the windshield, but she finally pulled the right lever that opened the hood. After checking that no traffic was coming, Georgie joined him at the front of the car. Her parents had gifted her the car for graduation, so it was only a year old.

"Do you know what you're doing under here? Or are you just trying to look like a hot mechanic?"

Jamie glanced over at her. "I am a hot mechanic. Or I was. My grandparents owned a garage in Jersey. My dad's a mechanic. I used to work there until I graduated high school."

Georgie looked at him with a whole new level of interest. "Wow. So you're more than just a pretty face."

He laughed but also looked a little embarrassed. From the little he'd mentioned about his parents, and what she'd overheard that night in the hotel, she knew his family was a sore subject. She hoped he didn't think she was poking fun at him. People often assumed she was a snob because of her family's wealth, but Georgie knew that having money didn't make her better than anyone else. As King often said, it was just an accident of fate.

"I think that's really cool. No wonder you're so successful. You've been working and fixing problems your whole life. Unlike me who didn't even know how to open the hood thing."

He glanced over at her. "I knew you didn't know how to open it."

"Whatever. So, is my car dead? Should I plan the funeral?"

He looked back to the maze of metal under the hood. Georgie wasn't sure how he could tell what was what.

"Not quite. It doesn't look like you popped a fan belt or anything else that would explain the smoke. But it could be anything. Maybe an electrical issue. These fancy foreign models definitely aren't my specialty."

"Thank you for coming to get me."

He kissed her forehead. "Of course. Wait in my car while I call the tow service."

Georgie retrieved a few things from her car before climbing into the passenger side of his SUV. It was another half an hour before the tow truck arrived. By that point, she wished she'd just taken a bath instead.

"What's wrong? I'm sure your car will be fine." Jamie said before pulling out into traffic.

"Nothing. I was going to the pharmacy, and since I never made it there I still don't have what I need."

"What do you need? We can pick it up."

"Um... it's girl stuff."

"Georgie, we're adults. If you need tampons, let's go get tampons."

"Not exactly."

"Spit it out, woman!"

"We've had so much sex that everything hurts. I'm not used to doing it every day. Okay? Are you happy?"

Jamie's chuckles only made her feel more self-conscious. "Stop laughing. I'm in pain over here."

He grabbed her hand. "I'm not laughing at you, I swear. You're just so shy about certain things, but then you'll grab my dick like it's nothing. I find it fascinating."

That made her smile. "It doesn't have to make sense."

"Okay, I don't think we need to go to the pharmacy. I have exactly what you need."

Georgie let her head fall back against the headrest. "It better not be your boner."

"*I* have to admit that I'm pleasantly surprised, Mr. Hamilton. I didn't actually think you had the cure, but I feel better already."

Jamie took another bite of ice cream and put his feet up next to hers on the coffee table. They were snuggled under a cozy throw blanket watching Netflix.

"But is it better than sex? That's the real question."

Georgie pointed the spoon at him. "Don't ask questions if you aren't ready to hear the answer. Considering that it feels like you broke my vagina, I don't think you want to hear my answer right now."

He winced. "Fair enough."

A phone rang, and they both looked around.

"That's mine." Jamie placed his bowl on the coffee table and paused the show they were watching. Georgie watched as he picked up his phone, made a face, and then put it in his pocket. He stood there, staring off into the distance.

"Is everything okay?"

No answer. Georgie had seen him look like this a few times before. Whenever she asked who it was, he'd always said it was his mother and then changed the subject. He'd never answered the calls or responded to a message that she'd seen.

She put her ice cream down and got to her feet. When Jamie still didn't move, she walked up and wrapped her arms around his waist.

He jolted, but then his hand reached down to cover hers. "How did you know I needed that?"

"You always look so sad after she calls." Georgie knew it wasn't her place to ask about his personal business but when she'd seen how lost and alone he looked, all she'd wanted was to comfort him. Jamie seemed to live his whole life avoiding intimate connections or anything more committed than a passport.

But spending these past few weeks together, even if it was in secret, she'd gotten to see a different side of him. He wasn't cold and remote at all. In fact, there was a deeply passionate man beneath the corporate exterior. She just wasn't sure whether he'd meant to show her that side or not.

"I'm not trying to pry but if you ever want to talk about it, I want to listen."

"Why?" Jamie's voice was rough with emotion. "I don't even like thinking about them. Why would you want to?"

"Because I know that if they created you, they can't be all bad."

When he didn't say anything, she assumed he wasn't going to answer. But then he sighed.

"My parents only call when they want something. Usually it's money. Not always though. This time my dad wants me to co-sign a loan for him to start building racecars."

Georgie paused. He'd told her his father was a mechanic, so she wasn't sure if the idea was something he was thinking about or if he was just tired of them asking for money.

"Does your dad know anything about building racecars?"

"No. He never does. Every year he finds some new scheme and becomes convinced his ship has come in. But my mom usually ends up asking me for the money, and it's really hard to say no. I hate disappointing her. She always supports his crazy ideas."

"That's a good thing, I guess?" Georgie thought it sounded nice to still believe in the man you'd married, even years later.

"It would be if my father cared about anyone but himself. I made the mistake of thinking he cared when he tried to warn me away from marrying my college girlfriend, Sheila." He looked uncomfortable.

"King told me you were married before. He didn't like her much."

Jamie shook his head. "No one did. My father begged me not to marry her. We weren't married a week before she was trying to add herself to my bank accounts."

"At least your father tried to warn you. That's good, right?"

"I thought so. Turns out he was only concerned because he could tell what she was up to. I guess one scammer recognizes another. He knew that if she got her hands on my trust, then he'd never see a dime of it."

"I'm sorry, Jamie." Georgie truly didn't know what to say.

She'd heard about his brief marriage before, but getting information out of King was like kicking a brick wall.

"That's why I won't marry. It's not fair to any woman to be shackled to my family. And I don't need to marry just to get the money in the trust. I'll let it go to charity. I have my own money. It's better than having my father constantly asking for it, too."

"So they're manipulative."

"That's one word for it."

"I'm sorry. That sucks. But you know that has nothing to do with you, right? You're a good son. And I'm sure they love you, even if they don't show it well. Look at your name. They wanted to name you after your father and keep that connection going. Obviously, they were proud to have a son."

Jamie smiled. "My mom told me she wanted me to sound fancy. Like someone who mattered. She always used to say that Jim Junior may be just a mechanic from Jersey, but James Hamilton III could be President."

"Well, if they wanted a son who mattered, they got their wish. Their son is kind. That's all he needs to be to matter. And if he ever changes his mind about marriage, he'd be a great husband. The kind who would respect his wife and treat her right."

Jamie pulled her closer, resting his head on hers. "If your vagina wasn't broken, I would show my appreciation. But we can just cuddle."

Georgie looked at the clock on the microwave in the kitchen. "I really need to go. It's getting late."

"Why don't you stay over? I can take you home in the morning."

The thought of going to sleep and waking up in his arms was so tempting. But if she allowed herself that, it would be even harder to return to sleeping alone when he left.

"I prefer sleeping in my own bed," she replied, ignoring his skeptical look at the weak excuse.

"One of these days I'm going to wake up with you again, Georgie. When there's no catastrophe to deal with and we don't have to rush you home."

As Georgie followed him out to his car, she decided not to remind him that he would be gone before that could happen.

Chapter 11

*J*amie slammed the folder he was finished with and threw it on the pile with the rest of the reports he'd just read. He hadn't been getting his usual satisfaction from work lately. Being at the office had never felt like an inconvenience before.

But that was before he started spending so much time with Georgie.

He groaned and buried his head in his hands. Even when he tried not to think about her, he ended up thinking about her. Every night they spent together brought them closer and closer.

Until the moment when she had to leave.

The moment he remembered that he wasn't supposed to be enjoying this quite so much.

It hadn't been obvious at first, but now he could see it so clearly. The sex wasn't why he was so obsessed with her. It was all of it. The way she listened when he talked about his day. How he looked forward to all the weird little observations she made about the world. Her scent. The feel of her in his arms.

He enjoyed spending time with her even when they were doing nothing. He just enjoyed being with her. Which was exactly what he'd promised not to do. The past few days, he'd pulled away from her and spent more time at the office. He had to break the dependency. But it hadn't worked. If anything, he missed her even more.

"Hey, you ready?"

"What?" He looked up to find King standing in the doorway to his office.

"Thanksgiving dinner? Tonight. At my parents' house. Man, where is your head this week?"

Jamie gripped the pen in his hand a little tighter. He was pretty sure *on your sister* wasn't the right answer to that question.

Luckily King hadn't seemed to notice the source of Jamie's distraction. He realized then that his friend was still talking and he hadn't heard any of it.

"Anyway," King continued. "Olivia isn't that close to her parents, so we definitely won't be splitting most holidays. I'm glad we're in town. I really need to check on Georgie."

Don't say anything.

Don't ask what she's been doing.

Don't do it.

"Why? Is she okay? Has Alex been bothering her?"

King shook his head. "No, she seems fine. I just haven't had much time to spend with her lately. Are you okay? You've been here even later than usual this week. I'm not the one to tell anyone else they work too much but... I think you work too much."

He laughed because that was what the old Jamie would have done. The one who had his shit together and wasn't pining after a girl that wasn't even his.

Who had never been his.

"I'm okay. Just tired. Yeah, let's go to dinner."

He could feel King watching him closely as he put on his suit jacket and grabbed his briefcase. He followed him to the Kingsley mansion, thankful that the traffic was light that day. Now that he knew he was going to see Georgie, all the parts of him that had been sulking earlier were suddenly wide awake. As they pulled into the long drive leading to the house, Jamie realized it was the first time he'd been back there since the wedding.

King let himself in the front door with his key instead of waiting for a staff member to open the door. The house smelled like pie and was tastefully decorated as usual, but none of that registered. He barely heard King greeting his girlfriend or Fiona coming over to say hello. The only thing he saw was Georgina.

Always Georgina.

Jamie kissed Fiona on the cheek and shook hands with Mr. Kingsley before crossing the room to where Georgie was sitting on the couch. She looked up at his approach and then back down at her hands. The only sign she was happy to see him was the blush on her cheeks and the little smile she gave him before she coughed to cover it.

"Hello, James."

Jamie smirked. If she was trying to keep things incognito, then she was failing miserably. She never called him James.

"Hey, princess."

She glanced around nervously. "Don't call me that!"

"Why not? He sat right next to her and leaned back, stretching his hand over the back of the sofa. Her long dark hair was resting behind her and he twirled a few strands around his finger.

"You know why. Someone could overhear."

He wanted to say that he didn't give a fuck if anyone overheard them. That she was his and he didn't care who knew. But then he saw how distressed she looked, and he sat up, removing his arm.

"You're right. I wouldn't want anyone to get the wrong idea."

"We'll probably be seated together at dinner, but I trust we can be civilized for that long. Besides, I have to leave soon anyway."

"Oh, hot date?"

He'd been joking but when she shrugged, everything inside him stilled.

"Something like that. Excuse me." Then she stood and gracefully walked out of the room.

"James, would you like a drink?"

He looked over at Mr. Kingsley's question and nodded. "Yes, sir. I could use one."

He was going to need alcohol to get through this dinner.

———

*H*e had another drink with dinner. And then another with dessert. Georgie had left by then, excusing herself from the table with a quick kiss for her mother and a wave to everyone else. No one questioned why she was leaving early, so he guessed she'd told them beforehand about her date.

He ground his teeth just thinking the word. By the time dinner was over, he already knew he wasn't going anywhere.

"You should ride with us, buddy. I think you had one too many at dinner." King clapped him on the back.

"I'm just going to sleep it off in one of the guest rooms if your parents don't mind. I don't really feel like going home. It's not like there's anyone waiting for me."

King's expression was unreadable, but Fiona immediately ushered him toward the stairs.

"Of course, you can stay over. Thane and I are going out tonight to visit friends and won't be back until late. They throw quite the party. But it'll be nice to know that Georgie isn't by herself in the house when she comes home. I hate leaving her here alone."

In his slightly inebriated state, Jamie almost laughed. Not only because Georgie was a grown woman but because the Kingsleys employed live-in staff. None of them were ever really home alone.

An hour later, the house was quiet. King and Olivia had left first, followed by his parents. Jamie had stayed over many times in the past but never with the express purpose of waiting up for Georgie. He felt a little guilty getting trashed so he'd have an excuse to wait for her, but desperate times called for desperate measures.

Georgie was out there on a date with some guy. He was just drunk enough to acknowledge that he was insanely jealous.

What they'd agreed on weeks ago seemed ludicrous now. How had they thought they could go from being lovers back to chatting about the weather? He knew how fast she splintered apart when he tongued her nipples.

There was no going back to basics after the things they'd shared.

A little while later, he woke up to the sound of footsteps. Blearily, he sat up and shook his head to clear it. He must have fallen asleep while waiting for her. He glanced at the watch on his wrist. It was just after eleven o'clock. Not that late by most people's standards but practically the middle of the night for Georgie. He'd come home with King many times to find her in her pajamas by ten o'clock reading a book. She liked to go to bed early.

But apparently her hot date had been worth staying up late for.

The thought of it guided his feet down the hall and to her room. He opened the door as quietly as possible. Her back was to him as she kicked off her shoes. Most of the bedrooms were actually suites consisting of a small sitting room and then an attached bedroom and bathroom. Georgie's sitting room was done in soft shades of rose with elegant crystal accents. It looked like her. Perfectly elegant. And way too good for him.

"You're back."

Georgie shrieked and dropped her handbag. "Oh my god. Jamie, what are you still doing here?"

He pointed at his face. "Had one too many. Was sleeping it off. Don't drink and drive."

"Well, you get points for safety at least. But that doesn't explain what you're doing here. In my room."

"Just checking on you. Your mom wanted me to watch out for you. She worries about you being here alone."

Georgie rolled her eyes. "As if I'm ever alone in this place. You know I don't need a babysitter."

"I know. I wanted to find out how your date went."

Her expression closed up instantly. "Fine. Besides why would you want to know about that?"

"Well, I was your first practice guy. Maybe I wanted to know if you applied what you learned."

As soon as the words left his mouth, Jamie instantly wanted to call them back. It was one thing to be pissed off and jealous, but he'd never been mean. That sounded like the kind of thing his father would have said to his mother during one of their famous arguments. The kind of thing he'd heard as a kid that made him feel shitty even when he was too young to understand what the argument was about.

Georgie was across the room so fast that he couldn't even track her movements. But the crack of her palm across his face got his attention.

"Fuck, that hurt."

"Good!" she yelled. "You deserve to hurt after saying that."

"Yeah, I do. That was a shitty thing to say. I'm sorry."

Her chest heaved with the force of her breaths and Jamie was instantly horrified to see tears on her cheeks.

"Sorry doesn't fix everything." Georgie said with such quiet dignity that he instantly fell in love with her. Fell deeper in love with her.

Because he was no longer fooling himself that the way he felt was a new or sudden thing.

"I'm jealous, okay? There, I admitted it. So jealous I can't see straight."

Georgie pointed at him. "*You* are the one who said we couldn't get attached. You are the one who has been blowing *me* off the past few days. Back to usual, remember? Everything was supposed to be the same as always."

"Except I can't stop thinking about you."

Now that he was telling the truth, it was impossible to stop. Somewhere in the back of his brain, he recognized that pouring his heart out while slightly drunk probably wasn't the best idea but the rest of him was on board with the plan.

Or at least it was better than continuing to bottle it all up and spending his nights miserable and alone.

She paused. "You can't?"

"No. And I don't even want to. I don't want to go back to normal. Normal sucks. I can't hide how I feel for you anymore. And I definitely don't want to go back to the way things were."

Chapter 12

It was a struggle to decide whether to kiss him or slap him again. After the night she'd had, she wasn't surprised she'd snapped. James watched her warily before rubbing his cheek.

"You pack quite a punch, princess."

"Only when necessary," she shot back trying to ignore the way her palm was stinging. She couldn't believe she'd actually hit him.

Slapping people was the kind of thing she'd thought only happened in the movies. Or on overdramatic soap operas.

Then again, she'd never had anyone make her as crazy as Jamie did so there was that. He had her behaving in all sorts of ways that were out of character. Sneaking around, defying her parents, going out without underwear.

It was a scandal!

She laughed at the thought, and Jamie's eyes narrowed.

"You're enjoying this, aren't you, princess? Is it funny to see me acting like a madman? Because that's what I feel like. Just the thought of you with someone else makes me crazy."

It was tempting to draw out the suspense a little longer, but she couldn't do it. She didn't want Jamie to think that she was out dating or sleeping with anyone else. Especially not when the only man on her mind lately was standing right in front of her looking like a bull about to charge.

"I wasn't on a date. Not really. I was catching up with some friends. Before that, I was with Alex."

When his nostrils flared, she realized how that sounded. "To give him the ring back!"

Jamie ran his hands over his face. "I'm not sure if that makes me feel much better. You should have sold it. Payment for all the time you wasted on him."

Secretly, she kind of agreed but when her mother had suggested giving it back, she'd decided it wasn't worth the fight. There was nothing she needed from Alex Summerland

and that included a diamond. She could buy her own diamonds, damn it. And those would probably mean more to her in the long run.

"I don't want anything from him. In fact, I think I'll buy myself something pretty to celebrate not having to put up with him anymore."

Jamie chuckled. "That's my girl."

She wished that was true. It was getting harder every day to keep him firmly in the *annoying friend of my brother* category. It was difficult not to look at him differently or rush to his side when he showed up with King for dinner.

Now that she knew how he smelled, how he tasted and how intoxicating it was to be the center of his laser-sharp focus, it was excruciating to pretend that he was nothing more than a family friend.

"I hate that you even went to see him," Jamie admitted quietly, looking like it pained him to do so. He pulled her close and held her against his chest.

Georgie relaxed, feeling the hard thump of his heart beneath her ear. She wasn't sure what was happening. His intensity made it seem like he was mad at her for being around Alex, but the way he held her made her feel cherished.

"It was nothing. I gave him the ring back, he tried to tell me how sorry he was, and then I left. His excuses were as stupid as I thought they'd be, but I'm still glad I went. I got the closure I needed so I can move on."

"That's the part I don't like."

"What part?" She leaned back so she could see his face.

"The moving on part. Dating other men. I don't want you moving on to anyone but me."

When their eyes connected this time, Georgie felt it in her core. She swallowed, suddenly aware the tension she'd read as anger was the same untamed passion he'd loosed on her during their sex-fueled night. He wasn't mad, he was turned on. And her body responded as if he'd sent up a mating call.

"Jamie, you said we would only do this until your trip. That we would keep it casual."

His lips feathered over her forehead gently and she shivered as the sensations tingled down her spine, spreading warmth.

"And how is that working out for you?" Jamie whispered.

"Not so well. Unless, waking up horny every night is normal."

His chest shook from his laughter. "You never fail to surprise me, Georgina."

"What? Too real for you?"

He shook his head. "I don't know if you're ready for how real I want to get with you. Just this room brings back memories."

She frowned. "My room? When have you ever been in my room?"

"I haven't been in here. Just caught a peek a few times when you would answer the door. You don't know how many fantasies I've had that began with you answering that door wearing your robe. Or nothing at all."

Suddenly his smile turned predatory.

"Oh no. Jamie, we can't! My parents could come home."

He shrugged out of his jacket, letting the fabric fall to the floor in a heap at his feet. Then his fingers slid under his tie. "Then I guess I'd better put something in your mouth to keep you quiet then, huh?"

It only took her about three seconds to make her decision. Yes, she was still mad at him. Yes, he was definitely a jerk for sneaking into her room and demanding answers he wasn't entitled to.

But she couldn't deny that she would have felt the same if she'd heard Jamie was out on a date. Even if it wasn't the smart decision, she wanted him again. They could worry about not getting attached later.

Although Georgie was pretty sure it was already too late for her.

"This is probably a good time to admit that I'm not wearing underwear."

Jamie's head snapped up, and then his hands went to work on his pants. "It's a really good thing no one is home, then. Because there's no way this is going to be quiet."

———

*H*e was a bad influence. There was no longer any doubt about it. Because as many times as he'd dreamed of being in Georgina Kingsley's bedroom while she undressed for him, he'd never in a million years actually thought it would come true.

Who said miracles didn't happen?

"I can't believe we're doing this," Georgie whispered. Her cheeks were bright red as she tugged down the zipper on her dress. "What if someone comes home? I can't look my mother in the eye and pretend I don't have a naked man hidden in my bedroom!"

Her outrage only made the situation funnier.

"Your parents are out for the night. King went home. The

only reason I stayed behind is because I had a few drinks and he thought I was plastered."

"So you're saying you duped my poor, gullible brother so you could put the moves on me as soon as we were alone?"

He paused unbuttoning his shirt to think about it. "I'm okay with that interpretation."

Then he tugged the shirt off and dropped it on top of his pants. Georgie stepped out of her dress and he wanted to howl when he saw that she was indeed completely naked underneath.

"I'm not sure I love that Alex got to see you like this."

She shook her head. "He can look all he wants but this isn't for him. It's for me. I like feeling sexy. And I like not having panty lines."

"I like you not having panty lines, too."

She snickered at that and then touched the waistband of his boxers. "I'm glad you stayed over."

He groaned when she pulled the band away from his skin, so she could fit her hand inside. As soon as her fist closed around his cock, everything that was wrong in the world instantly became right.

"Believe me, you aren't as glad as I am. That feels amazing."

She pushed his boxers down and then waited while he stepped out of them.

He lifted her carefully and walked back toward her bedroom. She fit so perfectly in his arms. He loved how her long legs wrapped around his waist as they kissed.

He bumped into the wall, sending Georgie into a fit of giggles before they finally made it into the bedroom. They tumbled onto the bed, their mouths locked together, her lush curves undulating beneath him.

"Jamie. Please. I want you."

Hearing that was like pouring gas on a fire. Then she took his hand and led him right where she wanted him. Her blue eyes fluttered shut as he slid one finger deep, already lost in the feel of her.

The pleasure of touching her was almost enough to make him lose it but he needed to be inside her again first. He looked up, not wanting to miss a moment of watching her fall apart.

Spending so much time together over the past few weeks had only sharpened the longing. Everything he'd felt before had been trebled. Georgie was more than just a forbidden fantasy, she was flesh and blood. Fire and sass. So much better than a dream because she not only enticed him but challenged him as well.

Right then, in her arms, Jamie finally felt like he was where he was meant to be. As her fingers clung to his bare back and her hips rocked to meet his, they were in perfect sync.

"You are everything dreams are made of. My perfect princess." His arms tightened beneath her, and he knew she'd probably have bruises later. But in that moment, his body was operating on its own wavelength. It knew what he needed, which was to touch and taste and hold. Tangible reminders that this moment was real.

"I'm not a princess," Georgie moaned. "You make me sound like this helpless thing that can't take care of herself."

"You are not helpless. I'm in awe of you all the time. Anyone else would have cried if their wedding day was ruined but you didn't make a scene, just did what you had to do. You started a business all on your own and you're a friend to everyone you meet. If that's not a princess, it's a fucking queen."

Georgie's smile washed over him like sunlight and was just as warm. "Oh, Jamie. What am I going to do with you?"

Choose me.

Stay with me.

Love me.

It was right on the tip of his tongue. But it wasn't something he could ask for or push her toward before she was ready. All he could do was wait.

And hope.

Georgie pulled him down for a kiss, her fingers tangling in the hair at the nape of his neck. It sent shivers down his spine. He loved the feel of her hands roaming all over him. Lost in the sublime experience of all her enticing dips and curves beneath him, he was completely unprepared when she angled her leg around his hip and flipped them over.

"Surprise," she teased.

"Nice surprise. I always enjoy this view." His hands immediately went to her breasts, cupping the soft weights and thumbing the sensitive tips. Now that she was in control, her hips swung seductively, rubbing her hot, wet center directly over his cock. No matter how he twisted or canted his hips, she kept herself just slightly out of reach but still managed to grind all over his lap.

"If your aim is to torture me, I give up. You can have whatever you want."

She grinned triumphantly. "My aim is to drive you crazy. As crazy as you make me." Suddenly she stopped moving. "Wait. I have to get something."

He watched curiously as she hopped off his lap and went into the bathroom. The view of her shapely ass bouncing as she ran off was worth the inconvenience of being left temporarily with a hard dick.

Georgie came back with a box of twelve condoms held over her head like a trophy. She posed with it a few times before climbing back on the bed next to him. James found himself smiling at her silly antics. If anyone had ever told him he'd be smiling in the middle of sex he wouldn't have believed it. But that was Georgie.

"I bought these just in case." She wouldn't meet his eyes but the blush rising from her chest to her cheeks gave her away. "May I?"

When he realized she was asking to put one on him, he nodded quickly. His cock hardened, like it knew it was about to get stroked. Georgie looked up at him and then tore the wrapper open. By the time she'd worked the rubber all the way down his length, James was painfully aroused and they were both breathing hard.

"I need you to ride me, princess. Right now."

Although her eyes widened slightly at the command, she threw one leg over him and lowered herself slowly down. Georgie panted with every inch deeper and it was a struggle to keep his hips still. But once she'd taken it all, Jamie couldn't hold it anymore. His hips canted upward and they both cried out.

"Jamie!"

His hand came up to cover her mouth. She bit his finger playfully before drawing one digit deeper into her mouth. It was the most erotic image, Georgie riding him and sucking his finger at the same time. One that he knew he'd never forget.

"I don't want you dating anyone else," he growled.

She nodded. "Okay. And that goes for you, too. This is all mine now."

His jaw clenched when she tightened her internal muscles around him. "Fuck yeah, it's yours."

Georgie's eyes glittered as she rotated her hips again, and everything went into slow motion. "Good. Because you're the only one I want, Jamie."

"Then I'm yours, princess. And I'll give you all you can take. Then I'll give you some more."

He flipped them over, lifting her thighs up so he could get deeper, the move changing the angle and making the fit even tighter. Georgie's head thrashed back and forth on the pillow as she started to come.

But then she opened her eyes and whispered his name. Just

once. *"Jamie."* And he lost the little bit of control he had and groaned out his release.

As Georgie let out a small, satisfied sigh, Jamie quickly took care of the condom, disposing of it in the trashcan in the bathroom. Then he climbed back under the covers with her, cuddling against her back.

There was a small part of him that wished that things could have been different.

If he'd made his move sooner.

If she hadn't met Alex.

But if all he could have of Georgie right now was her body, then he would take it. Because Jamie was used to working hard to get what he wanted. And if he had to bide his time until Georgie was ready for more, he could do that.

Chapter 13

*J*amie was the first to wake up, and it took him a few minutes to figure out where he was. Light gray walls. Snow-white comforter. Gorgeous brunette.

Bingo.

He was clearly still dreaming.

As much as he wished he could hang around and enjoy a leisurely morning with Georgie, that wouldn't be happening while they were in her father's house. Mr. Kingsley liked him, but no father liked a man who was rolling out of his daughter's bed in the early hours. He needed to get his ass up and out of here before anyone else in the house woke up.

"Georgie," he called softly. "Wake up, princess."

She whined and then rolled in the opposite direction. Georgie was adorable when she was tired and grumpy. He wished he could just let her sleep, but he didn't want there to be any other miscommunications between them. With his luck, if he left a note it would get caught on a gust of wind, sucked out an open door, and then eaten by a feral cat. As unlikely as that was, it was exactly the kind of thing that would happen just to screw with him.

"I have to get out of here before your dad catches me."

"My dad said what?" Georgie sat up straight, her hair flying around her head.

"Your dad hasn't said anything yet. Hopefully he'll never have to if I sneak back into the guest room without anyone catching me."

"Right. Yes. You should do that."

Jamie stood and searched the room for his slacks. Then he remembered that they'd both undressed in the sitting room. He leaned over and kissed Georgie before pointing to the other room.

"Don't get up. Go back to sleep. I'm going to get my clothes and get out of here."

"Okay. Is it weird to say, call me?" Georgie was adorably flustered.

"Not at all. I'll definitely call you. We're not going to do this sneaking around shit much longer. Which means I need to talk to your brother."

She made a face. "Any chance we could just ignore the problem for as long as possible and hope he never notices?"

"Uh, no."

"I was afraid you were going to say that. Okay, go be all responsible and stuff."

He hesitated briefly, wishing they were at the point where he could tell her how he felt. It seemed strange to just leave her without acknowledging that he would in fact miss her every moment until they were together again. But he had to remember that Georgie was in a very different part of her life. She'd just gotten her freedom back and probably wasn't ready to hear anything that heavy. This whole situation was going to require some finesse.

"Bye."

Determined to ignore the awkwardness, he walked back into the sitting room stark naked. His clothes were still in a pile in the middle of the floor next to the dress Georgie had been wearing. Her shoes were next to the chair and her handbag was on its side with stuff falling out.

What a story this picture told.

He'd just pulled up his boxers when the door to Georgie's room opened and King stepped inside. They both froze, looking like two animals caught in headlights. Then King turned around to face the other way.

"Put your fucking clothes on, for fuck's sake!"

Jamie almost fell over yanking his trousers up his legs. His shirt was next, and he was still buttoning it when King finally turned around.

"Should I even ask how long this has been going on? I should have known something was going on with you. The later than late nights, the attitude, the drinking. It's because you're sneaking in and out of my sister's room at night? Christ, James. She still has the tan line on her finger from her engagement ring!"

The door to the bedroom behind him opened. Georgie came out wearing an oversized T-shirt. "Would you keep it down? Or are you trying to wake up the whole house?"

King scowled. "No, I'm trying to find out how long my best friend has been screwing my sister."

Georgie crossed her arms. "Why does everyone think they have the right to know my business? You. Mom and Dad. The gossip rags. No matter what I do, it's never enough. Guess what, King? It doesn't matter because it doesn't concern you."

"It does concern me because I'm your brother and I don't want anyone taking advantage of you when you're down."

Georgie laughed. "Is that what you think happened? Maybe I just wanted to have some fun. Alex has a mistress. Why can't I have a booty call, too?"

Jamie put a hand over his chest, shocked at how much that hurt. He didn't think she'd even meant it the way it sounded but damn if that wasn't a wake-up call.

"Your brother is right. I shouldn't be here." He fixed the last button and then shoved his feet into his shoes. Georgie followed him as he walked to the door.

"King can shove it," she muttered. "Sorry about this."

"No, I was leaving anyway." He took her in, trying to imprint the moment on his memory. She was so beautiful even wearing an old shirt with no makeup and a pissed-off expression on her face.

"What? Why are you looking at me like that?" she asked.

"You really stood up to him," he said, angling his head toward King. "Which is good. I think that's what you need. Not only to prove that you can handle things to them but for yourself."

"Thanks. That's exactly what I want to do."

"Then do it." He held her face gently, his thumb brushing

back and forth over her cheek. "Go out there and do all the things you've always wanted to try but were scared of. Be brave. Be goofy. Be Georgie. People won't know what hit them."

She stood on tiptoe to kiss him. Conscious of King staring daggers through them both, he lingered over the kiss for just a moment.

"Take care of yourself, Georgie."

He didn't look at her as he left.

One look was all it would take to render him unable to leave. And walking away was the right thing. Not just for Georgie, but for both of them.

When he opened Georgie's bedroom door to walk into the hallway, Fiona was passing by. She looked at him and then at the bedroom door behind him in surprise.

"Oh, hello, James!"

"Good morning, Mrs. Kingsley." He died instantly observing the moment when she realized why he was coming out of her daughter's room.

"Thank you for your hospitality."

Fiona smiled, a bit too widely. "You're *always* welcome to visit, dear."

Jamie didn't even want to decode the meaning behind that statement. Especially if it meant what he thought it did. Apparently the Kingsleys weren't *that* obsessed with bloodlines if Fiona wasn't upset about him being with her daughter.

That was a worry for another time though. Because he had an entire schedule to rearrange and a trip to prepare for.

He finally knew what he needed to do.

———

Georgie watched him go, unsure why she had the sudden urge to follow him and hold on tight. Something about the way he'd just kissed her was different. It had felt... final somehow.

And she wasn't sure why.

"Do you have any idea what you just did?" King asked.

"Are you still here? Why?"

She was being rude but then again, so was he by invading her space this early in the morning. The clock on the wall said it wasn't even seven in the morning. Which made her wonder why he was even there in the first place.

"I was here to ask your advice on how to propose to Olivia since you're usually up early. But that doesn't matter now."

She turned to find King watching her with a blank expression.

"Why wouldn't it matter?"

"I'm not sure I want love advice from someone who could just stab a guy in the heart the way you just did."

Georgie's mouth fell open. "What are you talking about?"

"James is in love with you."

When she scoffed, King put up a hand. "You haven't worked with him for years. Spending that much time with someone, you get to know them. Even the things they think you don't see. He's always had a thing for you."

"I'm not sure I believe that. He's turned me down before," Georgie admitted.

It still stung that the only reason Jamie had been in her bed was because they'd discovered a mutual sexual compatibility and he was a guy so completely happy to be offered casual sex. They'd never had a relationship outside of the bedroom, and even last night he hadn't said anything had changed. He'd merely said he missed having sex with her and that he didn't want her with anyone else.

But that didn't mean he loved her. Alex had been possessive that way, too. It just meant he didn't like sharing his toys.

"That man cares for you," King insisted. "He probably didn't think you were ready before, but clearly he thought so now. I'm not sure why since he just had to listen to you call him a piece of ass."

"I did not!" Georgie couldn't believe her own brother was ganging up on her like this. Not that she'd wanted him to blame Jamie, but it seemed like King was more concerned about his friend's feelings than hers.

But then she thought back to everything she'd said. Although her first instinct was outrage, she could see how her words could come across as callous. But that was only because King didn't know anything about her relationship with Jamie. He knew nothing of their deal or that they'd both agreed to keep things casual.

And she wasn't about to enlighten him.

"Booty call wasn't the best choice of words, but Jamie is hardly a prude."

King sighed. "You didn't see his face when you said it."

Georgie shifted, wondering if maybe the comment hadn't come across as lighthearted as she'd meant it. Jamie had been a little abrupt as he'd left. But she'd chalked that up to embarrassment at being caught by his best friend.

Guys were so weird about the "sister" thing. Jamie was probably giving her time to reassure King she hadn't been taken advantage of or whatever boneheaded thing her brother had decided on.

All at once, the night without sleep caught up with her, and she was finished trying to decode the male mind. If King wanted to argue about her hypothetical relationship, he would be doing it by himself. She was going back to bed.

"I'm really tired. I'll see you later. At a normal hour." Georgie rubbed her eyes. Her brother could see himself out since he'd had no problem inviting himself in.

"You're going back to sleep? You're not going to apologize?" King stared at her incredulously.

"For what? You are the one who came in my room uninvited. If you saw anything that traumatized you, it's your own fault."

King looked like he wanted to strangle her. "Not to me. *To James.* To the guy who left here looking like he just lost his best friend. Which is really interesting because until recently, I was his best friend. You might want to think about what that means."

Chapter 14

*A*s soon as Jamie got home, he walked straight through to his bedroom. If he was going to Europe early, he had a lot of preparation to do. He hated doing things on the fly but considering what had just happened, it was best for all if he was on the other side of the ocean. He wouldn't have a chance to say goodbye to Georgie, but maybe that was for the best.

Booty call.

He shook off the hurt and tried to focus on what his next twenty-four hours would be like. Once he was in the office, he'd have a better idea of what meetings could be pushed forward or back. But he knew that getting out of town was for the best.

He heard the door open behind him and paused in the act of

throwing shirts in his suitcase.

"Who let you in? Someone's not getting a Christmas bonus," he said over his shoulder.

"I'm on your approved visitors list, asshole." King responded.

"I didn't think I'd see you this soon. Figured you'd need some time to cool down. Maybe put your fist through a wall first."

"I thought about it," King replied.

"Unless that's why you're here. You want to take this outside? Hell, I'll give you one shot for free."

Jamie didn't realize he was holding his breath until his chest started to hurt. He had known that King wouldn't approve of him with Georgie since the beginning, but that didn't make it any easier to hear.

They'd been best friends for so long that Jamie honestly didn't know what he'd do if King didn't forgive him. Would that be the end of their decade-long friendship? The end of their business partnership?

Damn, he'd really fucked this up.

"I might take you up on that. You owe me one to the face just for not locking the door. That could have been my dad knocking, you know."

Jamie grimaced. "Maybe the universe is looking out for me after all. I would have never been able to look him in the eye again."

When King didn't say anything, he figured it was time to put it all out there. He couldn't pretend he understood how his friend felt because he didn't have any siblings. But if nothing else, before he left he could try to explain and hopefully save some semblance of their friendship.

"I'm not sorry for loving Georgie. That would be like saying I'm sorry for being blond. She's a part of me."

He could hear King walking around the room. Finally, he chanced a look behind him and saw his friend staring at the diploma hanging on his wall.

Jamie kept it in his room as a reminder, but not for the reasons people would assume. The money his grandparents had left for him had been the difference between getting his degree from a prestigious school like Georgetown or having to settle for whatever school he could afford with loans.

After a lifetime of watching his father try one get-rich-quick scheme after another, Jamie had been determined never to have to ask anyone for money. He'd decided to study business so he could learn how to make money in legal ways.

But it had always been about proving that he could do it.

Growing up with parents who were constantly scamming for money had taught him the importance of acquiring it on your own terms. He'd promised himself that one day he would be somebody. Well, he'd succeeded. And it still hadn't been enough.

His parents only called when they wanted something.

Despite having more money than he could ever spend, he came home to an empty apartment.

All along, he'd been playing the game to win without asking what was the prize. Because the only thing he really wanted wasn't something he could buy.

Jamie moved to the next drawer in his dresser. "I'm going to Europe early. I might need you to cover some of my meetings next week."

King didn't try to argue or change his mind. But he did look disappointed. "She really didn't mean it the way it sounded. I know she feels really bad about it. You should talk to her. Let her apologize."

"No apology is necessary. Georgie doesn't have a mean bone in her body."

He had no doubt that Georgie had just been joking around when she called him a booty call, but unfortunately it had hit on all his old insecurities. That a woman like Georgie would only see a guy like him as fun for a night. It had forced him to take a step back and acknowledge he was in this thing a lot deeper than she was.

The last thing he wanted was to get trapped into a loveless marriage like his parents. His dad had left and come back so many times and for what?

Just to hurt his mother again.

"Aren't you supposed to be warning me away from her? You've never made it a secret that you don't think I'm good enough for her."

King actually looked shocked. "That's not true. When I found out you were with her after the wedding, I was worried. But not about Georgie. She dodged a bullet. I just wanted to make sure it didn't hit you instead."

"Too late," Jamie muttered.

Going back to sleep proved futile, so Georgie finally got up and went downstairs. Her father was already at work, but Fiona was in the dining room. A cup of coffee and a bowl of cut fruit were placed in front of her.

"Darling, there you are. I trust you slept well?"

Georgie sat in the chair next to her mother and poured herself a cup of coffee. "I did. It was fun to get together with the girls again. And I was able to meet up with Alex beforehand and give him the ring."

Fiona pursed her lips and took a dainty sip from her coffee cup. "I'm glad it's done. Distasteful as it was, it's better to make a clean break."

"Yeah, I guess it is. I'm just sorry you and Dad had to be embarrassed in front of all of your friends."

"No one was embarrassed except for the Summerlands. I know I've been hard on you Georgina, but it's only because I want you to be happy. I worry about you. Ever since you were a little girl, you've always been so impulsive. The world isn't always kind, and I wanted you safe with someone who could look after you when we're gone."

"Mom, I don't need looking after. Okay, maybe I do some-times, but that's only because I'd never had to learn how to do certain things before. But I'm learning now."

Fiona put her cup down gently in its saucer. "I can see that. You're much stronger than I was at your age. Fearless."

Georgie was shocked at the pride in her mother's voice. "I

always thought you were ashamed of me. Or maybe wished I was more like your friends' daughters. Elegant and ladylike."

"I wasn't always the perfect lady myself," Fiona confided. "And I've learned over the years perfect ladies don't get nearly as much accomplished. Being perfect isn't as important as being happy."

Her mother's look turned calculating.

"Perhaps our James will be a part of that."

Georgie almost spit out the sip of coffee she'd just taken. "What?"

"I saw him on his way out this morning. Darling, I must say that I always thought you two would make a striking couple. But you seemed to bicker like siblings, so I thought perhaps I was seeing things that weren't there."

Georgie was still stuck on the *I saw him on his way out this morning* part.

"Um, sorry about that, Mom. Oh my god, please tell me Dad wasn't with you when you saw Jamie leaving." Every part of her wanted to melt with shame at the thought of her father running into her lover in the early hours.

"No, your father was still getting dressed. Your secret is safe with me."

Georgie left her mother with a kiss before retreating back to her room. She needed to call Jamie and warn him. Because Fiona's version of a secret was taking out a billboard ad. She had to warn him before her father found out.

———

*S*everal hours later, Jamie still hadn't called her back. Finally, Georgie gave in and texted King. She wasn't inclined to ask for his help with anything after their fight that morning, but she was getting desperate. All she kept imagining was Jamie being cornered at work by her father, demanding to know his intentions.

Cringe.

King finally texted that he was coming over, which seemed a little odd. All of the men in her life were workaholics, so she knew they'd all gone in to the office today, even if it was the day after Thanksgiving. Why wouldn't her brother just walk over to Jamie's office and tell him to call her?

As soon as she opened the door an hour later and saw her brother's face, Georgie knew something was wrong.

"Hey, sis. Can I come in?"

"Now you ask?"

He narrowed his eyes at her. "Trust me, I've already paid the price for my mistake."

Georgie walked away, leaving the door to her room wide open. King stepped over the threshold and shut the door behind him.

That door was the start of the problem. If it had been locked, King wouldn't have been able to walk in without knocking. It wasn't King's fault, but it was convenient to blame him, so she was going with it.

"Your feeble brain will have to deal with it. I almost got married. How are you still shocked that I'm not a virgin?"

"No comment. Anyway, I saw Jamie earlier. He wanted me to tell you that he's going to Europe early. He'll be visiting some of our subsidiaries and visiting potential new partners. It's an important trip, and someone from Kingsley has to do it every year."

Georgie just stared at him. He was rambling. Her brother never rambled.

"He's already gone, isn't he?"

King nodded somberly. "Yes."

She rubbed her forehead, trying to make sense of everything. So much had happened today that it was difficult to keep track. But somehow, she'd gone from waking up with Jamie, to her mom giving her blessing, to King saying that Jamie was gone.

It was a lot to take in.

"Okay, but why did you need to tell me that? Why didn't he just text me?"

As the silence stretched out Georgie finally got it. Jamie didn't want to talk to her. That was why his kiss this morning had felt so different. Because he'd known then that he was saying goodbye for good.

"I think you need to give him some time," King replied finally.

"He's really that mad?"

"Words can hurt more than actions sometimes."

Such as right now, Georgie thought. Because hearing that Jamie would rather fly to another continent than see her again hurt worse than any physical blow.

"You know him better than anyone. What should I do?"

King sat on the small sofa in the sitting area. "It's hard to say. Jamie comes from a family that never thought he would amount to much. But now that he has, they only want to use him when it's convenient. So being referenced as a booty call had to bring up some unpleasant feelings for him."

Georgie wrapped her arms around herself, suddenly cold. These past few weeks with Jamie had been everything she'd ever dreamed of. Great sex and fun times with a man who believed in her wholeheartedly.

"I think I love him, King."

Her brother smiled kindly. "But you don't know for sure. And James knows that. Maybe it's time you stop thinking about being part of a couple and just figure out what you want. Just Georgie."

"You think I haven't tried that? This self-reflection stuff is harder than it looks." Georgie flopped down on the couch next to him and rested her head on his arm, the same way she used to when she was a little girl.

She looked up at him. Her brother might be a bossy know-it-all, but he always had it together and he'd found love with Olivia, so clearly he was doing something right.

"When you don't know what to do, how do you figure things out?"

King looked thoughtful. "It depends on what you're good at. Use your strengths in your favor. Your instinct will usually guide you in the right direction."

"Mainly I write things down. Or doodle. That's why I started

Sweet Nothings. But I'm not sure a greeting card will make Jamie come back."

"You'll figure it out. I believe in you." King made a disgusted sound. "Can't believe I just said that. All those Lifetime movies Olivia watches must be rubbing off on me."

"She's good for you," Georgie whispered.

"She's perfect for me. And maybe James is perfect for you. But you need to take some time to figure out if he is. Because if he's not really what you want, then it's best to let it go."

Chapter 15
SWEET NOTHINGS BY GEORGINA

It's been two weeks since you went away.

Not that I think you didn't know that, but I'm reminding myself. For once my brother actually had good advice. He recommended that I figure out how I communicate best and then use that to apologize.

So that's what I'm doing by writing you this note. I want to apologize. Because I would never in a million years want to hurt you.

Even though you won't answer my calls, you're still the first person I want to talk to every day. It feels like a million years since I last saw your face, but I still remember how you used to look at me like I was priceless. Maybe I didn't appreciate it enough until it was gone, but I miss it.

I miss you.

Yours,

Georgie

P.S. Since I don't know what country you're in right now, that's why I'm sending you an email. But here's a picture of the letter I wrote for you. Isn't it cute?

Chapter 16
SWEET NOTHINGS BY GEORGINA

It's been three weeks since you went away, and I really wish I could talk to you. Things have been bad here.

The gossip rags finally figured out the identity of Alex's mistress. They have pictures of him coming out of a hotel with none other than Regina the wedding planner.

I really shouldn't have been surprised. That woman put my bridesmaids in ugly dresses. At least I learned a valuable lesson.

Never trust a woman who likes eggplant.

On the other hand, all the media attention has been hard on the rest of the family. King has been working around the clock trying to contain it. My dad was just furious on my behalf. I think he was worried that I would be embarrassed. My mother had to take to her rooms after she saw the pictures. Regina was one of her oldest friends.

I expected to be hurt when I found out, but I really didn't care. Which was a nice surprise. I'm focused on more important things.

I thought about what you said to me that last day. About going after what I want and doing all the things that scare me.

For so long I wanted to do a line of angry greeting cards. Weird, right? But I feel like that's an untapped market.

Your best friend slept with your father? Your coworker keeps eating your tuna fish sandwich? I have just the card for you!

Look, I even composed the first card in honor of Alex.

Roses are red

Cheaters are blue.

So glad to be free

And by the way, FUCK YOU.

Kind of poetic, huh? I'll take a video when the new website goes live next week. I'm sure my mother will be so proud.

Yours,

Georgie

P.S. Are you really not going to answer any of my texts?

Chapter 17
SWEET NOTHINGS BY GEORGINA

It's been four weeks since you went away, and I still wake up saying your name.

Oh, and by the way, a picture of a half-eaten croissant wasn't the response I was looking for, but at least I know you're alive and haven't been kidnapped by European ruffians.

Or the Swedish bikini team. Which is probably more likely.

Anyway, I'm starting to feel like a bit of a stalker writing these messages that you never respond to (not counting the croissant), but I'm not giving up on us.

Is that what you thought would happen? Well, I'm here to tell you Georgina Kingsley is used to getting what she wants. I'm your princess, aren't I?

What we have may have started off casual but that's not how I feel about you, Jamie. This is worth fighting for. YOU are worth fighting for. So you'd better come home soon because I love you.

Yours,

Georgie

P.S. Don't make me sign you up for those stupid Furniture Barn emails again!

"elcome back, Jamie. We weren't expecting you in the office until next week."

Hesitantly, he took Mr. Kingsley's outstretched hand. It had been five weeks since what he'd started thinking of as "the morning-after disaster" but even so, he wasn't sure how the other man would feel. Considering how distraught he'd been at the wedding, Jamie had been expecting the cold shoulder. It wasn't like Mr. Kingsley wasn't aware Georgie had relationships, but that didn't mean he wanted to have the evidence up close and personal.

Even if it was a man he liked and employed.

"Thank you, sir. It was a successful trip, and we were able to wrap up early. I'm glad to be home."

When the other man didn't say anything else or ask to meet him on a grassy knoll at dawn for a duel, Jamie figured that King and his mother had opted not to tell the family patriarch about that fateful morning.

Small favors.

He waved hello to his secretary, who was already aware that he was back early, and then entered his office. It was odd to be back after weeks of visiting Kingsley's UK subsidiaries and potential partners. He'd been in London, Birmingham, Paris and Milan before visiting a few clients in Munich and Vienna.

This was the first year that the trip had been both an escape and a punishment. It sucked to be away from Georgie for so long, but it was the only thing that kept him from going to her too soon and ruining everything.

"So, you're finally back."

He didn't look up at the sound of King's voice. He'd figured once word got out that he was back in town, his best friend would be paying him a visit.

"I am."

"You were supposed to be gone for six weeks."

"This trip never really takes that long. It's an excuse to party for a few weeks at the end and get paid for it."

Jamie could tell King wanted to laugh and was struggling not to.

"Probably not something you should be telling your business partner who happens to be the son of the boss."

"Is that all we are now? Business partners?"

King crossed his arms. "Well, I thought we were friends. Until I found out you were banging my sister, *gross by the way*, and then you ghosted us all for weeks."

"Put that way, I sound like an ass."

"You won't hear me say otherwise."

"But that's not quite how it went down. I needed to go. Georgie and I, everything just happened so fast."

King held up a hand. "Don't need to hear that part."

"Right, anyway. She almost got married. To someone else. I don't think she was in the right frame of mind to make major decisions, so I made it for both of us."

Even though it had almost killed him to walk away.

"I know what she said hurt. Initially, I was on your side, but that was before watching my sister look more and more heartbroken week after week. You could have shut it down before you left. You didn't have to leave her hanging."

"Yes, I did. Because if I'd talked to her again I never would have been able to walk away. But I came back early because there's something I need here. And that's Georgie. I just needed to give her time to figure out if she really wants me, too. Or if I was just convenient."

King didn't look mollified but finally he pulled out his phone. "I don't really want to help you."

"I know. If you could choose a man for your sister, then I'm sure I wouldn't be the choice. But I love her, King. I love every goofy, crazy, weird thing about her and for some reason she seemed to feel the same way about me, too."

His phone went off and he pulled it out of his pocket. It was a text from King.

"You're texting me while you're standing right here?"

"I'm trying to help you. It's the address to Georgie's new office."

"Why are you helping me?"

"Anything is better than hearing you talk about being a convenient dick for my sister." King made a face. "Anyway, that's where she should be right now."

"I can't believe she has her own office now."

King shrugged, but there was pride all over his face. "Yeah. She said you encouraged her to do it."

"Nah, I can't take credit for this one. I just told her to go do all the things she always wanted to do but was scared to try."

It made Jamie smile. This was exactly what he'd wanted for her. To go out there and do big things. He only wished he could have been there to see her excitement when she'd done it.

"Well, whatever you said to her, it worked." King turned to go but stopped and turned back around. "And for the record, I don't have a problem with you being with Georgie. I always thought you had a thing for her. She needs someone who believes in her and someone who can keep her out of trouble. Not many men can handle that. So good luck, I guess."

Jamie burst out laughing. "A fine endorsement if I've ever heard one." But he recognized approval when he heard it. "Thank you."

"Don't mention it." King pointed at him, suddenly serious. "And I really mean that. Don't mention *anything* about what you do with my sister or what you think about doing. None of it. Still trying to bleach the sight of your hairy legs from my brain."

"Got it." Jamie smirked.

———

Georgie sat back and surveyed the new layout of her office. It was tiny and the window faced another building, but it was hers. She'd moved in the prior week and had been taking furniture deliveries every day. It was a lot of work getting an office set up, but she was determined to have everything in place before the New Year.

"Hey, future sister-in-law!" Olivia walked in carrying a large bouquet of flowers.

"Thank you. These are beautiful." Georgie took a quick whiff of the yellow roses and placed them on the edge of her desk. "So, what do you think?"

Olivia looked around the small space approvingly. "It looks great. King showed me the before pictures and I would have never thought this was the same place."

"The landlord gave me a rental credit in exchange for making some repairs and cleaning up the mess the prior tenant left behind. Do you want a tour?"

Olivia clasped her hands together. "Absolutely!"

Georgie led her back to the outer storefront. "We just got the bookshelves delivered today. I have display cases coming tomorrow. Since my new line of Revenge cards have been so popular, I decided to sell some of the bestselling verses on merchandise, too. So we'll have T-shirts, tote bags, and phone cases soon. It's finally coming together."

"King is crazy proud of you. And so am I. You've done such a great job. I can't wait to come here on opening day and buy some gifts."

Georgie felt the same tingle of excitement that she got every time she thought about customers coming in to buy things from her shop. *Sweet Nothings* had started as a random idea, a way to use her art and humor in a practical way. But it had become her lifeline. It was a passion that allowed her to channel all the emotion she didn't know what to do with. And it had allowed her to prove to her family, friends, and most importantly, herself, that she could handle anything.

"So, what are your plans for New Year's Eve? King and I are going to visit my parents. We'll probably visit some of my old friends, too. My old neighbors, the Alexanders, are throwing a party."

Georgie picked up the dust rag she'd left on one of the bookshelves and polished a spot. "I'll be at home. My parents are going to their house in Aspen as usual. I have a hot date with a glass of wine and the newest Stephen King novel."

"You're welcome to come with us," Olivia cajoled.

"I'm not going to be the third wheel as you and my brother suck face the entire time. He's so disgustingly in love with you."

Olivia held out her left hand to admire the massive five-carat rock on her finger. "The feeling is entirely mutual. Your brother is ridiculous. He knows I don't need a ring this big."

Georgie ignored a twinge of envy. "No, I will leave you two lovebirds to travel alone. We can get together next year. Maybe have dinner."

Olivia was quiet for a moment. "He still hasn't contacted you?"

"No. But I'm okay. I am," she insisted when Olivia looked skeptical. "I love him and sometimes it feels like there's a hole in the middle of my heart, but I'll survive. It turns out that I'm stronger than I look. I guess we just weren't meant to be."

It was true. Time hadn't made her miss him any less, but she'd learned how to function on her own. Christmas had been hard without him, but she had an active, full life. Her family was very supportive, and she had work that satisfied her creative instincts.

She refused to feel sad just because of the one thing she didn't have.

The bell over the door jingled merrily, and they both turned to look. A man stood with his back to them inspecting the front window displays. All she could see was a black coat and a black knit hat.

"Sorry, we're not open yet."

He turned around, and Olivia gasped. "Jamie? You're back!"

"Yes, I returned a little early."

"That's great. Georgie, I'll see you later." Olivia pulled her into a quick hug and whispered in her ear, "Something tells me you won't be spending New Year's with Stephen after all."

Jamie kept his eyes on her, not turning to look even when Olivia passed by to get to the door. The bell jingled again.

"Hello, Georgie."

She shook her head. "Hi. I can't believe you're back. It feels like it's been forever."

He looked around the room. "King told me about your store. That's great. I knew you would do amazing things if you ever had the chance."

It killed her that they were standing there talking like strangers. They weren't polite conversation. They were insults and sarcasm. She turned back to the bookshelves and focused on polishing. Clearly her letters to Jamie hadn't meant a thing if all he wanted to do was congratulate her on her business accomplishments.

"Thanks for stopping by."

His arms slid around her waist, and he rested his head on top of hers. Georgie instantly relaxed back into his arms. It was so familiar that she wanted to grab on and never let go.

"Please don't do this," she whispered. "It's been so hard with you gone. I was just now starting to get over you."

"Were you? Because I'll never get over you. No amount of time would be enough."

Confused, she turned her head so she could see his face. "Then why did you leave? It hurt so much every time I wrote to you and you wouldn't respond."

When he finally answered his voice was soft.

"I don't know the exact moment I fell in love with you. Somewhere between your sweet sixteen party and seeing you in a wedding dress. The exact moment is hard to pinpoint because it feels like loving you has been a part of me for so long."

"I love you, too," Georgie said. "That's why I wrote the letters. So you could be a part of my life even when you were gone."

Jamie cuddled her closer. "I know that now. But I had to leave to know for sure. I wasn't sure if you really wanted me or if I was just the anti-Alex. Princess, I'm a little older than you are, and I've had time to do what I want without anyone else's expectation. We got together so fast. I didn't want you to wake up one day realizing you'd never gotten to do anything on your own. I couldn't ask you to love me. I had to give you time to decide if you could love me on your own terms. If I hadn't left when I did, I would have never really known if what we felt was real."

"Well, I think that question has been answered," she replied. "I didn't want you just because you were there. I wanted you because of how you make me feel. But that doesn't mean I'm going to let you off the hook that easily. Expect a series of creative punishments."

Jamie laughed. "Thanks for the warning, but I expected nothing less. I plan on spending a lot of time making it up to you. In fact, Georgina Kingsley, will you go out with me on New Year's Eve?"

Georgie wanted to stay angry but when she really thought about it, she'd forgiven him as soon as he sent her the picture of the half-eaten croissant. Jamie would never knowingly hurt her. Everything he did was usually for her benefit somehow. Instinctively, she'd known that.

"I would love to go out with you on New Year's Eve. But why do we have to wait? Can't I come over tonight?"

He chuckled. "Nope. I want to take you out properly. We're going to do this right."

Georgie's heart soared, but she forced her lips into a pout. "I don't see why our old way was wrong. The old way was pretty fun."

He tipped her chin up until their lips met. "We'll get there. No rushing. We have a lot of time. Because I don't plan on ever letting you go."

*J*amie glanced at his watch again nervously. The wedding was supposed to have started ten minutes ago.

"Stop looking at your watch!" King growled. "You're making me nervous."

"Sorry. I'm sure nothing is wrong. Olivia probably just needed more time getting into her dress or something."

King glared at him. "My mom would have told me if that was all it was. What if she changed her mind? What if she doesn't want to marry me? I shouldn't have pushed her to plan this so quickly."

Colin rolled his eyes and went back to texting. "Bro, she's not leaving you. You're a douchebag, but she already knew that before she said yes."

King turned around, and Jamie stepped in between them to stop the impending fight. Just then the door to the hotel room opened. Mr. Kingsley stepped in. "How are we doing, fellas? Your mother said there was a problem with the bouquet, so they needed a few minutes to have another one made."

"See, there you go. Flower issues. Can we get this show on the road?" Colin stood, pocketing his phone.

Jamie clapped a hand on King's back to keep him in place. "We'll meet you guys down in the ballroom."

Mr. Kingsley and Colin filed out of the room, closing the door behind them.

"Why did I ask my brother to be in the wedding party again?" King asked.

"You didn't. Your mother did. It's tradition."

"Right. I should have just had you."

For his friend, that short declaration was tantamount to a love letter. Jamie nodded, trying to conceal how incredibly moved he was.

"Well, I've always understood you. Except for a few times."

King chuckled. "You mean when you thought you could secretly date my sister and I wouldn't find out?"

"Not my finest moment, I admit." Jamie adjusted the tie that had gotten twisted while King was pacing. "You look good. Olivia loves you. All is well."

King took a deep breath. "Thanks for talking me down. I'll be sure to repay the favor someday."

The words instantly brought to mind Jamie's most secret wish. To see Georgie in another beautiful white dress but this time walking down the aisle into his arms. They'd been taking things slow for the past few months. The trust and love he'd always known was there was growing. He would never want to rush her. She deserved this time to be young and unencumbered. He could only hope that one day he'd be lucky enough to call her his wife.

"I hope that happens for us one day. She's killing it with her business. She's thinking about opening another location. I want her to have the time to focus on herself first. In the meantime, I'm just happy to be a part of her life."

King followed him to the door. "It'll definitely happen. It has to. I need another brother. The one my parents gave me is defective."

"I'll make sure to mention that part when I finally propose."

King shrugged. "My sister is weird. She'd probably think that was funny. Whatever you do, don't assume you know what she needs. You've learned by now that Georgie has always danced to her own beat."

As they rode the elevator down together, Jamie thought about it. And started making plans.

---

*G*eorgie tugged on the hem of her dress. She'd gained a little bit of weight and it no longer fit properly. At least it was a flattering color, a blush pink with a sweetheart neckline.

"Stop messing with it. You look beautiful," Jamie whispered.

"The last time I was this stressed at a wedding, I was the bride." Georgie focused on keeping her steps matched with Jamie's.

If she fell and ruined her brother's wedding pictures, she would never forgive herself.

Her parents had paid an exorbitant amount to use the grand ballroom at the Fitz-Simmons hotel in D.C. Jamie had joked that it was a good omen since that hotel had been the start of many a love affair, including their own. Georgie figured her brother and Olivia didn't need luck.

Once they made it to the altar, Jamie went to stand next to King and she stood next to Olivia's friend, Serena, who was also a bridesmaid. Her brother had only had two requirements for the wedding, that it be small and arranged as quickly as possible. And of course, that they used a wedding planner who wasn't a family friend.

No one argued with him.

The wedding march started and everyone stood, but Georgie kept her eyes on her brother. She'd helped Olivia into her dress and had already shed a few tears seeing her friend so radiant and happy. Now she didn't want to miss her brother's reaction to seeing his bride for the first time.

When Olivia appeared at the entrance to the ballroom, King sucked in a deep breath and put a shaky hand over his heart. Georgie found herself getting emotional. Her arrogant, maddening brother had found the love of his life and Georgie couldn't be happier for him. When she looked over at Jamie, she found him watching her with a little smile.

Throughout the entire ceremony, he kept his eyes on hers.

Afterward, they followed the newly married couple outside to the gardens for the wedding photos. It felt like hours before they were finished and heading back in for the reception.

Jamie linked his arm with hers. "If I were to ever get married,

I wouldn't even need all of this. Just you, me and a pastor. Maybe we'd invite your brother."

Georgie blinked in surprise. Ever since New Year's Eve, their first real date, Jamie had been careful not to talk about the future. He was the best boyfriend, supportive and attentive, but he had this idea stuck in his head that she was too young to think about anything serious.

So it was surprising to hear him talk about a possible future wedding. Even though her first wedding had been a disaster, Georgie still wanted to get married. She wanted to stand up in front of her family and friends and declare her love for Jamie to the world. This time, she knew it was for all the right reasons. And most importantly, it would be with the right person.

"I would love to have a small wedding. Just our families. A few close friends."

Jamie stopped walking and pulled her into his arms. As always, they fit together perfectly. Georgie sighed as she rested her head on his chest.

"I want to marry you, Georgina Kingsley. But I want it to be completely right. So, one day, when you are ready, I want you to tell me. Just say when. Or send me a carrier pigeon."

"Really? I only tried that *once*. Can't a girl have a hobby?"

"I know you like to keep things interesting. Do we have a deal?"

"Deal. In the meantime, let's go watch my brother make a fool of himself dancing."

"By the way, King said I should mention that he approves. Apparently he thought that would help my chances."

Georgie laughed. "We'll let him think that. But just so you know, you didn't need any help. I think you got it just right."

They were both smiling as they walked back inside.

Epilogue
SWEET NOTHINGS BY GEORGINA

Do you remember the deal we made a few years ago at my brother's wedding? You said I should tell you when I was ready to get married.

Well, I'm ready. It's time to close this deal.

You have shown me the meaning of unconditional love. I finally understand why people say their partner is their best friend. I love you more than I ever knew was possible, and I cannot wait to be your wife.

Meet me at the altar?

Yours Forever,

Georgie

P.S. I hope you aren't disappointed there's no carrier pigeon. It turns out those things are REALLY hard to train.

———

I hope you enjoyed BAD BLOOD! You can find King and Olivia's story under the title BAD KING or at minxmalone.com/badking

Author's Note

Don't forget to sign up for my VIP list HERE for new releases, sales and free books!

Love Romantic Comedy?
Get ready for the most
inappropriate office romance ever!

NYT & USA Today **Bestselling Author**
M. MALONE

A USA TODAY bestseller!

I want this job.

And no one, especially not the office playboy is going to stand in my way. He's cocky and irritating and entirely too good-looking.

So WHY the hell did I just tell him my most shameful secret?

I want her.

Not sure what I did in my past life, but it must have been bad. Because the only woman I want is my co-worker.

My competition.

When I find out she's never taken a trip to O-town, we make a little wager. Not only will I win the client, but I'll prove to her that multiple O's are NOT a myth.

BEG ME is a standalone romantic comedy that will have you clutching your pearls and laughing until you almost choke.

Excerpt of *BEG ME*

© March 2018 M. Malone

MILO

"What just happened is I secured a multimillion dollar ad account for our agency. I just saved both our jobs."

She snorts delicately. "You just lied to a potential client and to our boss! Besides since when have you ever cared about *my* career?"

There it is again, the veiled accusation that I've hurt her somehow. I move closer, noticing how her eyes focus on my lips.

"Why would you think I don't care about your career? Tell me, I can see you're dying to since you keep bringing it up. What did I do that was so bad?"

That seems to take the cork out of whatever was holding her back. Arms flying, she gets all up in my face, and damn if it isn't the sexiest thing watching her march around while that clingy dress drapes around her.

"You stole the Adler account after I told you how much I wanted it! Six months. That's how long I spent researching them and planning for how we would approach them. And then James asks *you* to approach the client."

By the time she's finished, my mouth is hanging open and I'm experiencing something that I don't feel often. Remorse.

"Mya, I'm going to tell you something. And you probably won't believe it. But I need you to understand that I'm being completely genuine." I pause. "I'm a clueless jerk sometimes."

She crosses her arms. "I won't have trouble believing that."

"But you might have trouble believing that I didn't realize you wanted the Adler account for yourself."

Her eyes fire up again, but I hold up a hand before she can respond. "Just let me explain. When you first told me about the Adler account, I was already handling two other jewelers, remember?"

She nods reluctantly.

"We used to do that all the time, right? I'd see an account that I thought would be perfect for you, so I'd mention it. You'd do the same for me. We were friends once. Or at least, I thought we were."

The anger on her face has softened somewhat. "We were friends. That's why it hurt so much. I thought you knew how much I wanted that account."

"I truly didn't, but that's on me. Because that means I wasn't listening well enough and I'm sorry." Then, because I know it will make her laugh, I add, "but if it makes you feel any better Owen Adler has a serious flatulence problem. So you can take over those update meetings if you really want to."

Mya covers her eyes with her hands. "No, thank you. I got a little preview of that the last time he was in the office. Maybe the universe was doing me a favor in that particular case."

"Probably. So many things make sense now. I had no idea you wanted that account. No wonder you hate me."

Mya blushes. "I don't hate you. Not really."

The tension in the room goes down several notches, but I can sense that I'm still on thin ice with her. Not surprising since she's spent the last two years thinking I fucked her over on purpose. And she just saw me lie to our boss, a potential client and several of our colleagues.

"Look, this thing with the Lavin team is a win-win situation. He likes us and that's half the battle. Now that we're in, he'll schedule another meeting for us to present how we'd handle marketing for the new line."

"This is never going to work! Everyone knows we're not actually together."

It's amazing to me that she has this much faith in people after working in advertising for so long.

"Mya, have you forgotten what we do for a living? We make people see what we want them to see. People will believe whatever we tell them if we put on a show. Reality is what we say it is. If we say we're together, then we're together."

"And when people ask where my engagement ring is?"

"If anyone asks, we'll tell them we haven't found the perfect ring yet. Done. Handled."

She shakes her head and sits on the edge of the bed. "It's that simple for you, huh?"

I reach down and adjust the bulge in my pants which has been stuck at an uncomfortable angle ever since I kissed her downstairs.

"Believe me, nothing about this is simple. This is going to be the hardest thing I've ever done," I add putting extra emphasis on the *hard*.

She laughs but her cheeks darken slightly again. Damn messing with her is fun. It's so easy to get her flustered. Mya is such an interesting personality, equal parts ball buster and blushing schoolgirl.

"Don't think you're distracting me from the most important thing here. Who gets lead on the account?"

I grin, having known she wasn't going to forget that. That's my girl, all flash and fire and tough as nails. She might blush when I tease her, but she's not going to let anything slip by her. Mya loves to win just as much as I do, something that I never would have thought would turn me on in a woman. But competing with her is almost as sexy as the thought of...

She narrows her eyes at me as if she can hear my thoughts.

"We'll each come up with a full campaign to present to the Lavin team. That's usually what we do anyway, right? Well in this case, no one will know except for us who created each campaign. Mr. Lavin will choose whichever one he likes better and that's who will lead the account."

She appears to be thinking about it. "We let the work speak for itself. James is happy. The client is happy. I like it."

"It's the best way. Lavin Fashions deserves the best that Mirage has to offer and obviously that's going to come from either me or you." I sit on the bed next to her, noticing how she goes still.

"You really believe that?"

I nod. "Yes. We may not always agree on our methods but your work is exceptional, Mya. What you did for Fallen Angel Cosmetics was brilliant."

She smiles. "I liked your campaign for Murray's Tires, too. Who would have thought tires could be sexy?"

I laugh at that. "This is what I miss the most from when we were friends. When you love what you do, that's a reward in and of itself. But there's nothing like being able to share it with someone else. To explain the methodology behind why you made a certain design choice or went in a certain direction, and then know that they understand, it's thrilling."

Mya looks shocked and I'm suddenly self-conscious about being so open. But it's true, everything I said. That kind of synergy is definitely not something I'll find with the Brittanys or the Jessicas of the world.

That's something I've only ever had with Mya, actually.

"I like talking to you, too. Well, not when you're trying to drive me up the wall. But those other times, before everything. It meant a lot to me, too." Mya's eyes soften, like she's remembering, and I like that look on her.

While we've been talking, we've subconsciously moved closer to each other, and when she peeks up at me, she's so close I can feel her soft breath on my chin. All at once, she seems to realize how close we are and stands suddenly.

"I should go!"

"Not yet. Some of the Lavin team are staying on this floor, remember? We want them to believe we're really in *l'amore*."

Mya throws up her hands. "Well, how are we supposed to convince them of that?"

"For starters, they would expect us to share a room. They would expect us to want to share a room." I wiggle my eyebrows at her. "Maybe we should rock the bed and scream a lot."

I'm expecting her to laugh with me, maybe make a joke about

screaming my name. But instead, she just looks skeptical. Uncomfortable.

She shakes her head. "Like that's believable. That only happens in the movies."

"Are you saying you've never screamed during sex before?"

Now I don't want to overstate my case here, but I don't think it's a secret by now that I know my way around a woman's body. There are few things more satisfying than watching a woman lose hold of her inhibitions, melt against you and yes, scream your name. So when I see that look on Mya's face, the truth of the situation hits me in the face with all the subtlety of a two-by-four.

Prim, perfect Mya Taylor has never had that kind of sex in real life.

And every part of me is dying to know how that is possible.

Fuck me.

———

MYA

Considering how many things have gone wrong tonight, you'd think it couldn't get much worse. But apparently we haven't reached our quota on weirdness for the night. Standing in a hotel room alone with Milo while he talks about screaming during sex takes it to a whole different level.

Especially since the way he's watching me makes me feel he's not going to just let this go.

"Have you?" he presses again, his eyes locked on mine.

Which is not happening. I'm not talking about orgasms while he stares at me like that. Just not doing it.

"I'm hardly a virgin, Milo."

His face twists into a grimace. "Jesus, don't say that."

"What? I just said–"

"What you said was a bullshit attempt to deflect and not answer. Which tells me everything I need to know." He runs his hands through his hair looking pissed off. Which makes no sense to me.

"How did we go from discussing your bad behavior at dinner to talking about my love life?" *My non-existent love life,* I think ruefully.

A guy like Milo probably goes through women like underwear. What would he say if he knew it's been six months since I've been laid?

Or kissed. Or hugged. Or touched.

Great, now he's got me thinking about how pathetic I am.

"I'm just trying to understand what the fuck is happening in the world that a woman like you is having bad sex. Any man lucky enough to see you naked should be putting in the work to take you to O-town every time."

Something in my expression must tip him off because suddenly he stops pacing and stares at me. "Mya, you've *had* an orgasm before, haven't you?"

Now we've crossed the line from inappropriate to just straight-up embarrassing.

"Of course I have. Not that it's any of your business."

He still looks disturbed but at least he's no longer looking at me like some kind of space alien. Which is why I have no idea what possesses me to say what I do next.

"Just not while anyone else is there," I mumble softly.

"Fuck me!" he explodes before whirling around to blink at me in disbelief. His mouth opens and closes several times before he makes a strangled growling sound that has me going instantly wet. "Fucking hell."

"Fucking isn't the problem," I snap, mortification at what I've admitted starting to sink in.

Of all the people I could have confided in, why would I tell Milo? For years it's been my secret shame and the real reason my ex didn't want to "settle" with me. I've read every Cosmo article, tried yoga and hypnosis and even those weird-ass positions in the illustrated Kama Sutra I ordered online. William was so offended when I suggested using a vibrator in bed and he didn't even seem to like when I touched myself.

Maybe that was the problem. It all felt like work instead of fun. And right now, it just feels like one more way I don't measure up. Especially with the way Milo is looking at me.

"You know what? I'm done talking about this. This has been a long night and we're probably both going to be out of a job tomorrow once James sobers up and comes to his senses. So for now, I'm going to my room to get comfortable."

He springs forward and grabs my arm. "Wait, Mya. I'm serious about not leaving yet. I'm pretty sure Christiane is staying on this floor. And she seems predisposed to hate us anyway."

Fed up with being told what to do, I reach behind me and unzip my dress. "I need to get out of this bra before it cuts off my circulation." I raise my eyebrows, waiting to see what he'll do.

But he shocks the hell out of me when he calls my bluff. Milo grabs one of the discarded dress shirts from the bed and hands it to me. "Change into this. You can order room service and relax just as easily here as you can in your room."

Clearly, like most men, Milo has no idea what relaxation means for a woman. But I'm just embarrassed and exhausted enough not to care anymore. So I take the shirt and escape into the safe haven of the bathroom. Once the door is closed and locked behind me, I meet my own eyes in the mirror. That was the most ridiculous conversation, but in a strange way cathartic, too. Maybe I just needed to tell someone and Milo happened to be the unlucky bystander when it all came bursting forth.

Not that he should have acted like it was such a bother to him. I'm the one who's been sexually frustrated for years, after all. If anyone has cause to be annoyed by this situation, it's *me*.

The bathrooms in this hotel come stocked with all manner of toiletries, so I use the mini facial bar to wash my makeup off. There's a small hook on the back of the door, so I use that to hang my dress by the straps and put on the shirt Milo gave me. It's a good thing he's so tall or there would be no way this thing would fit over my chest, but it's just big enough. Although I have to unbutton quite a bit at the top so I don't feel like my boobs are being strangled.

After pulling the pins out of my bun, I finger comb my hair

down around my face. It's super thick, so it's easier to keep it braided or in a bun, but when I'm relaxing, I just let it go wild. Milo will just have to deal. He's the one who wouldn't let me leave, so if he doesn't like it, he can bite me.

The man looked like he wanted to bite you anyway.

With that thought, I yank open the bathroom door and march back out into the room. Milo looks up from the mini bar where he's selected a small bottle. His mouth falls open slightly before he clears his throat and looks away, guiltily.

"Want a drink?"

"Uh, sure."

"We have scotch, some dubious-looking wine and vodka."

I shrug. "Alcohol. Anything that can make me forget the past three hours."

He's about to respond when my phone rings. To my surprise, Milo picks it up as if he has every right to know who's calling me. He tilts the screen so I can see the face. A picture of me and William taken during our last New Year's Eve flashes on the screen. I take the phone and hit the button to silence the call.

"I never got around to changing the picture on his profile," I blurt. Then I'm instantly mad at myself for explaining. I don't have to justify why I have a picture of my ex on my phone.

"He's called twice already. Some men really don't know the meaning of no, do they?"

I climb back on the bed, satisfied when Milo's eyes follow the movement of my legs. He hasn't invited me to take over his bed, but oh well. This is what you get when you stand in between a girl and her chill time. I settle back against the pillows and snuggle into the cozy sheets.

"William wasn't too good at listening in general," I admit.

"Enough about him. What did you think of the rest of the Lavin team? Obviously Christiane hates us. But otherwise?"

To my surprise, for the next hour, we talk about everything related to Lavin Fashions. It's not a surprise to me that Milo has researched their prior campaigns but he also looked up human interest stories about the brand and found out what their charitable initiatives are. That's one that I hadn't thought of yet. Then I tell him about the collaborations Mr. Lavin did before he started the brand. That was something Milo hadn't thought of.

And in the midst of it all, I can't help thinking that we make a pretty damn good team.

"Can I ask you something?" Milo asks when there's a lull in

the conversation. We've been sitting quietly for a few minutes, but it's a good kind of silence. The comfortable kind where you don't feel any pressure to perform, you can just be.

"Sure. I mean you've already asked the embarrassing stuff, like how I like my orgasms. How much further down the rabbit hole can we go?"

His smile awakens something in me that I didn't know was dormant, and I press my thighs together to stop the ache. But as usual, Milo is tuned in to everything I'm feeling. His eyes drop to the juncture between my thighs and his blue eyes darken. When he speaks, his voice is one shade above a growl.

"Why did you stay with a guy who didn't satisfy you? One who made you feel that you had to wear long skirts and hide yourself? I'm trying to understand, but I just don't get it. You're so strong. I can't imagine you taking shit from anybody."

This is the kind of conversation we probably shouldn't be having when I'm dressed in only his shirt and snuggled next to him on a bed. Maybe it's the mini-bar wine stealing away the last fucks I had to give, but I just don't care anymore.

"Even strong women get lonely," I say finally. "Will isn't a bad guy, just an oblivious one. And he wanted something I couldn't give him. Do you know what he said to me at the end?"

He turns over so he's now facing me directly. "What?"

"He said that settling down with me felt too much like settling. Like I was the consolation prize he'd accepted when he couldn't find anything better."

If you'd asked me before that moment, I'd have told you I was over it and that Will's words didn't have any power over me. But saying it to Milo in that moment was different, like I could actually admit how much it had hurt.

"And now he's trying to get you back. You know why?"

I shake my head through the tears that have suddenly sprung to my eyes.

He tips up my chin. "Because he's finally wised up and discovered how lucky he was to even have a chance with you. A chance that he won't get again. You are one of a kind, Mya Taylor. And you are no one's fucking consolation prize."

The phone on the bed between us rings again and the picture of Will and me flashes on the screen. Milo looks down at the phone and then up at me. "May I?"

I have no idea what he means, so I shrug. He grabs the phone and swipes right to answer.

"Yes. No, you have the right number, this is Mya's phone. This is her fiancé."

My mouth falls open.

"That's right, her *fiancé*. A guy who is smart enough to know exactly how special she is and how lucky I am to be with her. A chance you won't have again, so please fuck all the way off and stop calling." He pulls the phone away, but then before he disconnects, he puts it back to his ear. "And by the way, pal, her kneecaps are *fantastic*."

Then he drops the phone back on the bed and his mouth crashes down on mine.

————

Download BEG ME now
at minxmalone.com/begme

The runaway bestseller that will have you clutching your pearls and laughing until you almost choke.

BEG ME

My cock a doodle doo is on strike.

Yeah I know, I can't believe it either. But he'll only crow for one woman. The competition.

Spoiler Alert *she hates me*

ASK ME

Am I arrogant? Maybe.

Do women love it? Abso-F'ing-lutely.

Then I meet the one woman who isn't impressed.

WANT ME *

*Preorder: minxmalone.com/news

BAD KING

My parents just put a gold diggers target on my back. But if all they want is a wedding, I can do that.

Who Wants to Marry a Billionaire?

Must be completely inappropriate.

BAD BLOOD

When my best friend's little sister gets left at the altar, I'd do anything to help her. Until she asks for the one thing I can't give. Revenge sex.

BLUE-COLLAR BILLIONAIRES

Inheriting billions from the deadbeat dad they never knew sounds pretty sweet. Until they find out what he really wants in exchange.

TANK / FINN / GABE / ZACK / LUKE

THE ALEXANDERS

One More Day / The Things I Do for You

He's the Man /All I Need is You

Say You Will /Just One Thing

- Bad King -

Co-authored with Nana Malone

Shameless / Force / Deep / Sin

* * Paranormal Romance * *

BROTHERHOOD OF BANDITS

Nathan's Heart / Ian's Fall / Gavin's Curse

About the Author

M. Malone is a NYT & USA Today Bestselling author of completely inappropriate romantic comedy. She spends most days wearing Wonder Woman leggings and T-shirts that she's embarrassed for anyone to see while she plays with her imaginary friends.

She lives with her husband and their two sons in the picturesque mountains of Northern Virginia even though she is afraid of insects, birds, butterflies and other humans.

She also holds a Master's degree in Business from a prestigious college that would no doubt be scandalized at how she's using her expensive education.

facebook.com/minxmalone

twitter.com/minxmalone

instagram.com/minxmalone

bookbub.com/authors/m-malone